Advance Praise for

MOVING THE PALACE

"Charif Majdalani has a ripping yarn to tell and tells it with a raconteur's bravura. Transporting, wholly engaging, deeply moving. This book is why I travel and why I read."

—Andrew McCarthy,
award-winning director, actor, and author of
Just Fly Away and *The Longest Way Home*

"On one side the desert, infinite, immensely varied, splendid. On the other, the courage, obstinacy, folly, violence, and dreams of men. Through this fascinating adventure, Charif Majdalani constructs one of the most beautiful epics I've ever read."

—Antoine Volodine,
author of *Minor Angels* and *Naming the Jungle*

"This novel provides entrée into the extraordinary fictional work of Charif Majdalani; with each book he lays out magnificent, terrible and true history through family genealogy, hopes and dramas. And each time Majdalani renews our vision."

—Patrick Deville,
author of *Plague* and *Cholera*

"In language of extreme classicism—he is often compared to a Lebanese Proust—Majdalani imposes his rhythm, slow and mesmerizing, to bring us in step with his story ... Throughout this epic tale he intimately weaves together the grand history of his country and his family, mixing fiction and reality in language of infinite sensuality."

—*L'Express*

"An odyssey in the manner of *The Thousand and One Nights*."

—*Le Figaro littéraire*

"An extraordinary book somewhere between adventure story, picaresque novel, fairytale and chronicle of a bygone era."

—*Neue Zürcher Zeitung*

"Recounts the immense folly and excess of an explosive colonial episode—forgotten, deadly, torturous and involving weapons traffic and hidden treasures. Something that would have excited the adventurer Rimbaud had he survived his injuries …. Flaubert … would have loved this imaginary depiction of a real historical event."

—*Le Point*

"The reader remains captivated long after having completed this epic and comic novel that allows one to perceive in the ineffable silence of the desert the attachment of a man to his homeland."

—*Le Monde*

"Full of stirring epic images, trenchant anecdotes celebrating the virtues of movement … Majdalani has a way of merging time and place that makes his writing convey the concerns of men, their illusions, the sounds of the desert and the rhythm of marches and halts."

—*Le Matricule des Anges*

MOVING
THE
PALACE

CHARIF MAJDALANI

Translated by
EDWARD GAUVIN

NEW VESSEL PRESS
NEW YORK

تمت ترجمة هذا الكتاب بمساعدة صندوق منحة الترجمة
المقدمة من معرض الشارقة الدولي للكتاب
This book has been translated with the assistance
of the Sharjah International Book Fair Translation
Grant Fund

Cet ouvrage, publié dans le cadre d'un programme d'aide à la publication, bénéficie de la participation de la Mission Culturelle et Universitaire Française aux Etats-Unis, service de l'Ambassade de France aux EU.

This work, published as part of a program of aid for publication, received support from the Mission Culturelle et Universitaire Française aux Etats-Unis, a department of the French Embassy in the United States.

MOVING THE PALACE

New Vessel Press

www.newvesselpress.com

First published in French in 2007 as *Caravansérail*
Copyright © 2007 Éditions du Seuil
Translation Copyright © 2017 Edward Gauvin

Cover illustration: Mahendra Singh
Book design: Beth Steidle

Library of Congress Cataloging-in-Publication Data
Majdalani, Charif
[Caravansérail. English]
Moving the Palace/ Charif Majdalani; translation by Edward Gauvin.
p. cm.
ISBN 978-1-939931-46-7
Library of Congress Control Number 2016915498
Lebanon—Fiction

MOVING THE PALACE

Strange man, bethink thee now at last to reach thy
high-roofed house and the land of thine fathers.
— Homer, *The Odyssey*, Book X

1

THIS IS A TALE FULL OF MOUNTED CAVALCADES BENEATH great wind-tossed banners, of restless wanderings and bloody anabases, he thinks, musing on what could be the first line of that book about his life he'll never write, and then the *click-clack* of waterwheels on the canal distracts him; he straightens in his wicker chair and leans back, savoring from the terrace where he's sitting the silence that is a gift of the desert the desert spreads in its paradoxical munificence over the plantations, the dark masses of the plum trees, the apricot trees, the watermelon fields, and the cantaloupe fields, a silence that for millennia only the *click-clack* of waterwheels has marked with its slow, sharp cadence. And what I think is, there may or may not be apricot orchards or watermelon fields, but that is most definitely the desert in the background of the photo, the very old photo where he can be seen sitting in a wicker chair, cigar in hand, gazing pensively into the distance, in suspenders, one leg crossed over the other, with his tapering mustache and disheveled hair, the brow and chin that make him look like William Faulkner, one of the rare photos of him from that heroic era, which I imagine was taken in Khirbat al Harik, probably just after he'd come from Arabia, though in fact I'm not at all sure, and really, what can I be sure of, since apart from these few photos, everything about him from that time is a matter of myth or exaggeration or fancy? But if I am sure of nothing, then how should I go about telling his story; where shall I seek the Sultanate of Safa, vanished from the memory of men but still bound up with his own remembrances; how to imagine those cavalcades beneath wind-tossed banners, those Arabian tribes, and those palaces parading by on camelback; how to bring together and breathe life into all those outlandish, nonsensical particulars uncertain traditions have passed down, or vague stories my mother told me that he himself, her own father, told her, but which she never sought to have him clarify or fasten to anything tangible, such that they reached me in pieces, susceptible to wild reverie and endless novelistic embroidering, like a story of which only chapter headings remain, but which I have waited to tell for decades; and here I am, ready to do so, but halting, helpless, daydreaming as I imagine he daydreams on the verandah of that plantation in Khirbat al Harik, watching unfold in his memory that which I will never see, but shall be forced to invent?

*

Yet his story, at the start, hardly differs from those of any other Lebanese emigrants who, between 1880 and

1930, left their homeland to seek adventure, fame, or fortune in the world. If many of them met with success thanks to trade and commerce, there were some whose stories retained a more adventurous note, such as those who braved the Orinoco to sell the goods of civilization to peoples unknown to the world, or those who were heroes of improbable odysseys in the far Siberian reaches during the Russian civil wars. He was one of these, who came back at last with his eyes and head full of memories of escapades and follies. Tradition has it that he left Lebanon in 1908 or '09. He could've headed for the United States or Brazil, as did most, or for Haiti or Guyana, as did the most courageous, or for Zanzibar, the Philippines, or Malabar, as did the most eccentric, those who dreamed of making fortunes trading in rare or never-before-seen wares. Instead, he chose the most thankless land known at the time, and headed for the Sudan. But back then, the Sudan offered immense opportunities to a young Lebanese man who was Westernized, Anglophone, and Protestant to boot. And he was these three things, the child of an ancient family of Protestant poets and littérateurs, originally Orthodox Christians from the Lebanese mountains, poets and littérateurs who, when the winds of revival wafted through Eastern philosophy, wrote treatises on the modernization of tropes in Arab poetry, whole *divans* of poems, and even an Arabic-English dictionary. Of his childhood, nothing is recorded; this much, however, is: at the age of eighteen he began his studies at the Syrian Protestant College in Beirut. After that, the ancient name he bore was not to open the doors to any career path other than a scholar's, attended by some unremarkable post in the service of the Ottoman administration. This, it seemed, would not suffice him. Like the conquistadors who left a Europe that could no longer contain them, he left Lebanon one spring morning in 1908 or '09, no doubt taking with him in a small suitcase a few shirts and handkerchiefs, and in his head a few delicate memories, the trees in the garden of the familial abode where a salt wind echoed the stately meter of the open sea, the aromas of jasmine and gardenia, the skies above Beirut vast and mild as a woman's cheek, and the liturgical whiteness of the snows on Mount Sannine.

✳

In those inaugural years of the twentieth century, the Sudan has just been retaken by Anglo-Egyptian armies, who put an end to Khalifa Abdallahi's despotic regime, and returned the land to Egypt. Confusion still reigns, the country is only half under control, the reconstruction of the ruined former capital has barely begun. But after decades of obscurantist tyranny, a new world is being born, and in the flood of men showing up to seize the still innumerable opportunities are a few from Lebanon: merchants, smugglers, artisans. But he is not one of these. The oldest accounts about the man who would become my grandfather report that he was a civilian officer in the Sudan, and it was in that capacity, no doubt, that he would live out the fantastical adventures attributed to him. Just as it reached Sudan, the British Army was in fact starting to recruit Anglophone Christian Arabs of Lebanese origin to act as liaisons with the local populace. Considered civilian officers, these intermediary agents were first assigned to the Egyptian Ministry of War in Cairo before being dispatched to their postings in Khartoum.

This means that at first—that is, the day he arrived in Khartoum—my grandfather had come from Cairo, after thirty hours of vile dust and soot tossed backward in black plumes by locomotives first of the Cairo-Luxor line, then the Luxor-Wadi Halfa, then the Wadi Halfa-Khartoum. Here he is, stepping off the train, covered in dust right up to the pockets of his white suit jacket, sand in his eyes and nostrils, the same amused air as in the photo I mentioned, with his trim mustache and Faulknerian brow, though for all that, hair neatly combed and suitcase in hand. For a *mallime*, a massive Sudanese man in white robes sees to dusting him off with a great feather, after which a British officer politely waiting in the wings steps forward to ask, "Mr. Samuel Ayyad?" And like that he is taken in hand, conveyed to the barge that crosses the Blue Nile, then to Khartoum itself, and then, in a carriage, through the construction site that is the city to a white, new, unfinished villa where he must make his way over piles of brick and goatskins filled with cement, getting his shoes all dusty again, though not with the usual brown dust, but rather the white powdery dust of plaster. "One of these rooms will be your office from now on, sir," explains the British officer. "You will share it with a colleague. The rest of the house will be yours."

*

So everything starts off wonderfully, and we will continue on in the same vein, imagining that the next morning the same officer takes him to Naoum Choucair, a Syro-Lebanese man of an older generation, advisor to the heads of the British Army. And with him, the contract is clear. "You will have two months to familiarize yourself with the country," says the old veteran, an adventurer from the age of Khalifa Abdallahi. "You will receive reports from different districts, and you will write up a summary of them in English. That will be an excellent exercise with which to begin." We will say that they are in Choucair's office in the buildings being restored in Gordon Pasha's former palace. Of course, the Nile can be glimpsed through the window, and when Choucair notices Samuel's furtive glances, he drags him toward it, declaring that this room is Gordon's former office. He points out the Nile's far bank, to the west, the train station where Samuel disembarked the night before, feluccas with their slanting masts on the river, then a seagull. Then there is a long silence punctuated by the din of laborers' hammers and trowels as they work on renovating a palace façade, and Choucair resumes his speech: "It will be an excellent exercise with which to begin. You will be assigned the office in Kurdufan, a district you will no doubt have reason to visit."

Samuel, who has returned to his wicker armchair, notices Choucair's hesitation. He sees the hesitation of the man now seated sideways on a little sofa, elbow on the back, he reads the question in the man's eyes, and anticipates it by nodding that yes, of course, he knows exactly where Kurdufan is. "At any rate," says Choucair after this little silent exchange, "I'll have a map of Sudan hung up in your office." He rises and heads for his desk, which is cluttered with books, manuscripts, letters, and strange instruments—spyglasses, portolans, even wooden statuettes he must have brought back long ago from the Bahr el Ghazal. He has probably occupied this office no more than a few months, but already he has layered it with the silt of a dozen years of travel across the land. He is of medium height, a bit tubby, with a graying beard, and the look of a great dreaming rover. What's more, he keeps getting up and sitting back down again, making sweeping gestures as he speaks, without a care for the bottles of liqueur, statuettes, vases he is constantly in danger of knocking over, as if he were more at ease in a pirogue on the Upper Nile or pitching on the back of a camel in the desert than confined by four walls. At that very moment he must be describing, per- haps by way of compensation, his famous and monu-

mental *History and Geography of Sudan*. From amidst the
disorder of his desk he plucks a cigar, offers Samuel one,
and begins to speak once more, not in English now but
Arabic, the Arabic of Lebanon; he claims to know well
the Arabic-English Dictionary of Nassib Ayyad, Samuel's father; he says this knowledge of languages is an asset
(he says "our knowledge of languages," and no doubt he
means we Lebanese); he says the British need people who
speak Arabic as well as they do English, and that proud
as Baring and Kitchener are of their officers who speak
Arabic, they speak like asses and understand even less,
they learned Arabic from *The Thousand and One Nights*,
and he laughs. Samuel smiles, watching him with curiosity, never interrupting, for from such men there is always
much to be learned.

*

"You will share this office with a colleague," the officer
said. But for now, he is alone in the villa still being built,
with the Sudanese workers in their white robes that grow
ever less white as the day goes on. They come and go
indolently, talk loudly, carry tools—goatskins on their
backs and planks on their heads—and mistake him for
an Englishman because of his complexion, his neat mustache, and his jovial air, as well as his English. He doesn't
disabuse them, for he wants to be left alone in the house.
Of course, he understands everything they say to one
another, but he remains impassive. Besides, all they talk

about is work, and sometimes among themselves they call him the Englishman or the Christian: out of the way, the Englishman's coming through, throw a plank over the mortar so the Christian can cross. His office is finished, there's already a table, chairs, and an armchair, and then one morning, a noncommissioned officer brings over a map of the Sudan. On the floor above, he sleeps on a camp bed, and this will not change before he leaves for Kurdufan. There is nothing else in his bedroom, and then one morning a little wardrobe and a hat rack are brought in. The villa overlooks the Blue Nile, and from the office window, Samuel can reach out with one hand and pick the fruit from a pear tree because, unlike the house, the yard has not yet been redone. It is still an uncultivated yard, like most former yards of the residences of Egyptian Khartoum which, before the city was abandoned, once served as gardens and orchards for the inhabitants of the Mahdist city. When he is not eating pears, he writes a few letters to his parents, or takes a walk in town, down new streets laid out with string from the Nile to the south, along which rise as yet unfinished white buildings. He wears a hat and a light gray suit with a little ascot, and meets British soldiers, merchants from Kurdufan, a few civilians in European attire, Greek or Armenian, Sudanese on donkeys and mules. He also goes for walks a bit farther south, in the jumble of former commoners' neighborhoods half in ruins, with their smells of rotting hay, traversed by sudden, bewildering empty lots left untouched since the city was deserted, whose abandonment would seem complete were it not for a mule-driver who suddenly appears and disappears just as swiftly in the opening at the end of an alley. He also goes, of course, to look at the massive project to the east that is the future Gordon College, and the former gardens of the Catholic Mission to the west, not far from the villa where he lives. And then, while sitting on his bedroom balcony over the yard, he spies Omdurman, the populous Mahdist city. It is to the left, in the distance, on the far shore of the White Nile, a brown and ochre mass with hundreds of boats on the river. He sees it and also senses, around him, the powerful presence of an enormous country that is half desert, roamed by tribes whom decades of holy wars, tyranny, and famine have wearied.

2

THE COLORFUL SNATCHES OF MY GRANDFATHER'S STORY that have survived are full of mounted cavalcades beneath wind-tossed banners, singular banquets, and baths in the middle of the desert. But you must imagine the prelude to all this: garrison life in Khartoum, with what must have been the sudden irruption, in our newcomer's life, of a kind of men he'd never had to associate with before—British Army officers. For example, Major Malcolm White, who knocks at the open garden door one morning. A Scottish officer, going by his accent, he turns up without any luggage, accompanied by an aide-de-camp, and introduces himself as my grandfather's future housemate, extending a generous hand while looking this way and that, surveying the lodgings. He vanishes into the house, climbs upstairs, and comes back down, seeming satisfied at last. He sits down, gladly accepts a cup of the coffee Samuel has procured from a Greek grocer, and speaks grumblingly, his words swelling and bulging in ways Samuel has a hard time understanding at first. He refers to himself as *Maucaum Wy*, calls Samuel *Mister Shawmule*, and when he speaks of Khartoum, Samuel thinks he is speaking of cotton. The next day, not only do his bags arrive, but also his furniture: a Victorian bed, a chest of drawers, a wardrobe soldiers have carried from a small barge on the Nile. Samuel soon realizes that after his departure the major will be the villa's sole occupant, but meanwhile, given the lack of habitable houses, he has been billeted with a civilian.

From this day on, at any rate, the aide-de-camp and the major's batmen graciously extend their services to include Samuel, who sees his breakfast brought up every morning to his bedroom balcony, and takes his lunch every other day at the officer's table. At first, Major White inspects him carefully, because this Syro-Lebnanese fellow who speaks such perfect English intrigues him. He ends up taking a liking to my grandfather, and brings him along in a British Army tilbury to the governor's palace, where Samuel finds himself once more in the large office in which, from morning till midafternoon, for several months, he reads, then summarizes in English, reports that pour in from all four corners of the country: from Suakin on the Red Sea, from half-ruined and deserted Al-Ubayyid in the middle of the desert, from the depths of the equatorial forest, as well as the steppes and their ancient, still-standing fortresses which all tell the same endless stories—tribes are marching toward southern Darfur, others have reached Wadi el Milk, an unidentified group attacked a caravan near Dongola, a Mahdist preacher has drawn a following in the *souqs* of Shendi and Metemma. At first he reads these dispatches quietly, deciphering the gesture-rich language of sheikhs and their scribes, the cramped and rigid tongue of Egyptian officers, the dialect of Nubian *omdahs* aquiver with local expressions unfamiliar to him, then he begins pacing from his table to the wall where a sometimes-incomplete map of Sudan is hung. He plants himself right in front of it for a few long minutes, tracing imaginary routes with his fingertips, then returns to his table and spreads out the reports, sorting them into piles, grouping them by region, theme, rubric, before gathering them all again and writing out his summaries. Once finished, he wanders home through the streets of Khartoum, where Nubians are busy planting slender tree shoots that will one day be jacarandas and, quite soon in fact, will sprout clusters of mauve blossoms beneath which prominent citizens of Sudan, with their massive hands, will pass in their sumptuous white turbans.

And then, at night, are the ritual gatherings in the villa's garden; my grandfather can't tell if these are part of life at the palace or the barracks. In the sonorous limpidity of the night, redolent at times of the Nile and at others of the desert, beneath lamps a generator allows them to use, but which they soon switch off for peace and quiet, they then light kerosene lanterns hung from pear tree trunks, drink Major White's whisky, and converse. They are, invariably, the major and his aide-de-camp, Naoum Choucair, and three or four of the less uptight

British officers, the less martial, the less racist garrisoned in Khartoum, among them a captain once stationed in China, another bored by the Old World, and a third in love with all things French. Now and again, birds perturbed by the light flutter in the trees; occasionally, suicidal insects hurl themselves like pebbles against the tables, and sometimes one will even dive into a glass of whisky. Then the captain once stationed in China will say he saw snakes and even monkeys preserved in brandy there, and swear he never tried a drop, calling for a new glass if indeed it is his glass the insect has landed in that time. But more often, the conversations revolve around battles in the Nuba Mountains, or skirmishes with the implacable Mahdist rebel Osman Digna in the region around Suakin. There are always unlikely tales to be heard, such that one night the lieutenant in love with all things French and recently returned from Suakin sporting a splendid seventeenth-century pearl-handled pistol of Ottoman manufacture, tells of how, during an ambush, one of Osman's old soldiers shot down one British soldier with it before tossing it like a boomerang at another, dealing him a mortal blow to the brow. The miraculous and sinister weapon is passed from hand to hand; Samuel feels the weight of it in the hollow of his palm and since, in the meantime, the others have begun telling tales of incredible duels, when his turn comes he tells the one about the Lebanese mountain man who one morning found himself face-to-face with bandits laying into two women and an old man. Despite the dust and rocks on the trail, the mountain man is on foot, with his cane and a floppy hat, when suddenly he hears shouting. He heads over and sees a mule braying in the middle of the path, a woman screaming, another howling for help, an old man struggling with two young hoodlums in *sirwals*. Without a second thought, Samuel continues, he rushes forward, whirling his cane over his head like a saber from the olden days, and routs the two hoodlums. But one of them must've gotten a hard blow to the nose, or some more sensitive spot, maybe between the legs, and his anger is such that he draws a revolver. The women's shrill cries grow even louder, they hold their heads in their hands like Aeschylus's beggar women, but the man, unruffled, walks over to the boy, stares him straight in the eyes without blinking, spreads his arms, lashes the air, and with a flick of his cane, Samuel placidly concludes, sends the revolver flying. A murmur of pleasure runs through the small gathering, and they take a swig of Major White's Old Parr, all the more satisfied because the tale was told with such astonishing brio. The officers ill-acquainted with him examine this Syro-Lebanese fellow with interest, naturally unaware that he hails from a family of poets and men of letters, nor of course that the tale he's just told is that of Nassib Ayyad, his own father.

*

If these evenings' invitees are selected from among the less uptight and less martial of the garrison's men, it is fairly uncertain at first whether Colonel Moore, under whom Samuel worked in the years that followed, is one of them. The two men meet for the first time during a reception at the governor's palace, one of those receptions that contrast violently with the low-lit vigils at the villa, notably due to the dazzling light pouring down on the great hall from two massive chandeliers the Madhi once had transported to Omdurman, which the English brought back after reconquest and restored to their former place, this time supplying them with electricity, such that the salon at this moment is no doubt the best-lit spot in all Sudan, and that, seen from the Nile where the feluccas of Sudanese fishermen glide, its windows seem an immense diamond in the midst of the night. Inside, the clamor is intense, cubes of ice more precious than gold make a crystalline clink in the whisky glasses, the wine itself is chilled, there are epaulettes on every shoulder while the Sudanese *sofragis* are flawless in their dignity, their sheer size silently conferring something royal on this military hullabaloo. Samuel attends this reception and is profoundly bored. He tosses back whisky after whisky and discusses French naturalism and English realism with Covington, the captain in love with all things French. On his way home in the tilbury, he tells Major White he won't be going to one of those evenings again, but three weeks later, it is Naoum Choucair who comes to his office specifically to tell him that he has been assigned to the staff of Colonel Edward Moore, in whose honor a reception will take place that very night to welcome him to Khartoum, and Samuel must absolutely attend. That night, no sooner has he entered the salon with White than Choucair takes him by the arm and leads him to the colonel, who is of course, surrounded by a palette of braid-trimmed shoulders and brightly decorated chests. Just as Samuel is shaking the martial hand of the guest of honor, whose gaze is immediately distracted by something else, Major White walks up, cigar in hand, and announces to Moore that he envies him for having someone on staff as remarkable as this young man. The colonel turns back from his distraction, gathers his wits from their wandering, and looks right into Samuel's eyes. Whereupon my grandfather experiences, for the first time, that shifting gaze he will have so much to do with, an ever-darkening gaze accompanied by a stiffness of feature on the whole and a hardness, even a cruelty, of expression that almost immediately relaxes, opens, and grows limpid, light gray, imbued with almost naïve kindliness.

For now, let us say that it is in its hard phase, a cold metallic hardness that quite simply plunges into Samuel's pupils and stays there, as if to gauge their internal pressure. But Samuel doesn't look away; with a polite word, he leaves his gaze open to Colonel Moore's predatory one. Immediately, the colonel's gaze changes, enters its retractile phase, brightens, and grows almost affable. And the officer speaks, probably says something like, "So you're the young man I was told about," or "Any young man both White and my friend Naoum Choucair (he pronounces it Choogair) recommend can only be of the highest order" (and with this, Major White and Choucair make little bows of false modesty and raise their glasses), or even "Such an appealing young man (and this time, it is Samuel who must, if not bow slightly, at least smile or make some gesture of acknowledgment, though he does not move), who speaks three languages—for you speak French, too, I'm told (and this time, Samuel is quite obliged to nod imperceptibly in assent)! Now that can be quite useful, quite useful indeed" (and maybe then, in a moment of wit inspired by the situation at Sudan's borders, he might throw in a little joke along the lines of "Now does he speak Amharic? If so, I resign!" and his eyes freeze, darken, as if a bitter memory had crossed his mind, then he softens and now he's even laughing at his own bad joke). He must say something of the kind, surely, after which—and this is the important part—he adds, locking eyes with Samuel again and launching the piercing arrow of his gaze into Samuel's own: "In a few days we leave for Kurdufan. Come see me first thing tomorrow. We must talk."

The next day Samuel goes to see him in a white suit with a handsome ascot and laced-up ankle boots, deliberately too civilian and too much the citified dandy, to remind Colonel Moore that he's no soldier, and that the somewhat rough attitudes at the heart of the hierarchy in no way concern him. For we can imagine that his first meeting with Moore has not left him with a very pleasant memory. But upon his arrival, he is greatly surprised. For when he presents himself at the ancient, recently restored clay-brick dwelling where the colonel is housed, he is made to wait a moment, then shown in and made to wait some more in a courtyard garden before a batman bids him follow. He crosses through ornately wood-paneled rooms with grand rugs and English armchairs, goes up a flight of stairs, and stops before a sculpted wooden door he is surprised to find the Mahdists haven't already carried off to Omdurman. When at last the door creaks open and a noncommissioned officer appears, then steps aside to let the two men in, Samuel finds himself in a vast room—giving onto a *mashrabiya*, covered with a few rugs, and furnished with a Damascene chest inlaid with mother-of-pearl—in the middle of which stands Colonel Moore, arms held straight out to either side. At his feet, a few Egyptian tailors bustle about taking in his shirt and pants cuffs, while seated in European wing chairs, forming a larger circle, English and Egyptian officers and even a civilian or two fill the air with chatter. Right when Samuel comes in, Moore exclaims, "Ah! There's our Lebanese friend!"

After which, during the entire week that follows, every morning when Samuel arrives at the colonel's residence, the latter is always busy, now with his barber, now with his armorer, now with his watchmaker, and every time, whether covered in shaving cream, a giant towel on his belly, from beneath which his hands leap and reach out in welcome, or else absorbed in inspecting a few American rifles (which Samuel thinks may be for the soldiers' use but not at all, they're for future gazelle hunts in Kurdufan) or new pocket watches a young Frenchman is presenting, seated across a rosewood table from the colonel as if for a game of checkers—every morning, upon seeing Samuel come in, the colonel lets out his unwavering "Ah! There's our Lebanese friend!" such that Samuel is finally put out. But he says not a word and, every time, merely takes a seat amidst the colonel's court, between two captains or beside a petitioner, a Greek shop owner, or an Egyptian broker or even, one morning, beside two camel drivers come to ask a favor concerning their caravan's route. They are sitting clumsily in their djellabas in the Empire wing chairs, and their henhouse stench is so obvious that Colonel Maher, an Egyptian advisor of Moore's, pulls a face and keeps bringing a handkerchief to his nostrils. Which earns him a sidelong glance from the colonel who, after dealing him the icy steel of his gaze, retracts it, relaxes it, and announces in booming tones, "Maher, drop that handkerchief, you're behaving like a demoiselle at one of Alfred Soussa's salons." Then he bursts out laughing, casting a complicit glance at Samuel, doubtless proud of this allusion to the upper-crust salons of Syro-Lebanese Cairo. Everyone laughs, and joins in with their own jokes, waiting as they do every morning for the colonel to finish getting himself a ceremonial outfit made to order, or getting shaved, or picking out a rifle, a watch, a pair of shoes. For only afterward does Moore begin hearing the officers on his staff and receiving complaints, responding to the soldiers' concerns, seeing to a case of Egyptian deserters, or another about merchants suspected of selling his regiment wheat with too many oats mixed in. He has a few notes taken by a lieutenant who sits down beside him, or refers an affair to his liaison services, then abruptly, unpredictably, gets to his feet before he's done listening to all the requests and reports, sometimes interrupting a lieutenant mid-sentence, and leaves, followed by his little court, with whom he'll call on the governor or tour the streets of Khartoum, on foot or in a calash along the Nile, and Samuel finally thinks that Colonel Moore acts less like an officer of the British Army than a bey in the Lebanese mountains, an Ottoman pasha, or a viceroy of the Khedivate. And then, one day, he is admitted into the calash that dashes along the banks of the Nile, and takes this opportunity to ask the colonel exactly what is expected of him. Moore turns to him, examines him with that open water lily of an eye, amiable and almost merry, and then, addressing Captain Covington and Colonel Maher across from him, declares laughingly, "Ah! Our young Lebanese friend is getting impatient!"

Then, speaking to Samuel once more, "We leave for Kurdufan the day after tomorrow, Mr. Ayyad. You've now met my entire staff. You have only to be ready."

3

THE VAST PROVINCE OF KURDUFAN, WEST OF THE NILE, is where the great Madhist revolt of 1880 first broke out, where hundreds upon hundreds of tribes rose up and followed Muhammad Ahmad, known as the Mad Mahdi, where the populations of whole cities and towns placed themselves at his service, forming a giant army with thousands of banners for him, endless civilians trailing in its wake, that swept the armies of Egypt and their British commanders aside and seized Khartoum in September 1882. Bound to the north by the desert, to the south by the Bahr el Ghazal, and to the west by Darfur, where the ancient sultanate was restored in 1900, Kurdufan is not yet entirely at peace when Colonel Moore's troops begin their march in spring 1910. Though the pitiful remnants of the tribes scattered or slaughtered by the Mad Mahdi's tyrannical successors have begun returning to their lands, their villages, which the 1890 famine emptied out, have never recovered, their cities lie in ruins, and above all, preachers calling for Mahdist purity have continued to rise up. And beyond a shadow of a doubt, another Mahdist uprising is behind Colonel

Moore's expedition, and thus Samuel Ayyad's departure from Khartoum.

That morning, Samuel, who has been furnished with a handsome mount and a second horse for his baggage, bids farewell to Major White and his aides-de-camp. He is in his army uniform, but without any insignia, and to emphasize that he is no military man, wears a paisley burgundy silk scarf, a gift from one of his sisters, knotted airily round his neck. His mustache is trim and his gaze jubilant. He leaves around ten, crosses the White Nile on a barge, and joins Colonel Moore's regiment a few miles from the river, heading south. Moore watches him arrive, waiting until he's ridden up the length of the column to exclaim, of course, "Here's our Lebanese friend!" and Samuel, concealing his annoyance, openly extends his hand as he draws abreast of the colonel, who after a moment of incomprehension takes it in his own. Then the two men ride side by side, ahead of Colonel Maher, whom Captain Covington graciously keeps company.

At first, the purpose of the campaign is uncertain, and the direction it takes undefined. Word arrives that a chieftain of the Nihayat tribe by the name of Moussa Bellal, a native of the western sultanates, has declared it his mission to retake Kurdufan and even the whole of Sudan. The hotbed of the revolt, the place where informers most often place Moussa Bellal, is at the foot of the mountains of Darfur. At first, the British task their allies the Kababish tribes with bringing the rebels to heel. But the volatility of Bellal's initiatives, his raids and appearances much farther east, then south, have driven headquarters in Khartoum to send out Colonel Moore after him. And so, at first, Moore leads his column west-southwest, to cover all the territories where Bellal is said to have been spotted. The first few days are flat as the landscape, and just as colorless. They skirt miserable hamlets, most often deserted, and market towns where half the houses, mud or brick, seem to have slowly melted, returned to the earth or subsisting in the form of dirt mounds or sculptures of sand. Now and again, by a well, a few rickety donkeys seem to be awaiting the hour of the resurrection and, upon a second glance, from the white spots of their turbans in the shade of the old acacias, donkey drivers can be made out squatting or sitting on woven mats, indifferent to the troops passing by. In the early afternoon, the colonel sends a group of soldiers on ahead, and when the column catches up to them at nightfall, they've already made camp, pitched the colonel's tent, prepared his dinner, and set out by the door to his transitory dwelling a rug, chairs, tables, and even a small escritoire of African manufacture, with several drawers. The officers gather, Samuel the only outsider. Dinner is spartan, after which Moore hears a few reports, then without further ado, goes to bed.

But things soon change. They enter the territories where Bellal is said to have been active, and have the sympathies of the tribal chieftains. No sooner does day break than horses and messengers set out ahead, east, west, and south, as if radiating from the column's advance in every direction, and at night, upon reaching camp, which has been pitched as per usual, not only are the colonel's tent, rugs, and furniture waiting but also four sheikhs from the Kawahla tribes, all in ceremonial garb: great white robes, imposing headgear, and swords at their sides, each accompanied by a small retinue. And this time, the meal is more sumptuous. Quails, partridges, pheasants served in sauce, gazelle chops, and then fruit, one after the next, while the colonel discusses with the sheikhs through the intermediaries of Maher and Samuel. They bring up Bellal, of course, but the chieftains swear they've never seen him, that they're faithful to the government, and that they've had enough of war and poverty. When Moore asks them if they're ready to help him in the event of an encounter with Bellal, they say yes, without hesitation. Everyone is satisfied then, and continues the meal, sitting at a table set in the middle of the savannah. Lanterns light the feast and the long shadows, the crimson of the rugs tossed on the sand, the rigid soldiers waiting on them and the soft murmur of the encampment all around lend the scene a royal allure. And this royal aspect will keep leaping out at Samuel's eyes. The next day it's the same thing, groups riding on ahead to organize everything, others riding out to round up tribal chieftains, but this time the column arrives first and waits. Nefaydiya chieftains arrive next, one after another, like biblical Magi, on camels and bearing gifts, acacia honey, dates and date syrup, mutton fat; and dinner is served. Instead of wine, date nectar and perfumed water flow from ewers of silver or brass. Shortly before the chieftains arrive, Samuel remarks to the colonel that receiving these Sudanese at a table is not quite appropriate. Moore's eye abruptly hardens, then relaxes, and that night, the banquet takes place on the ground, on rugs. They eat, elbows on cushions. They talk of the Mahdist rebellion and Samuel thinks himself in some Orientalist dream. The next morning, however, the troop inspection is fearsomely strict. We have returned to the heart of Western army discipline, the Oriental satrap is back to being a British colonel, and reviews the troops with a scowl; then a captain reads out the day's agenda, and once more it is all about England, Egypt, the future of the world, of civilization, of order in the Sudan. When they leave this time, Moore, riding beside Samuel, engages in a bit of chitchat—very five o'clock tea—then brusquely changes tone and asks him what he thinks of Colonel Maher. And since Samuel remains quite discreet, the colonel gives him that unyielding look: "Don't take me for an idiot, Mr. Ayyad. You've noticed perfectly well that he translates my conversations with the Sudanese chieftains quite carelessly. He doesn't like them. To him, they're all former Mahdists. He makes no effort. And he could've warned me earlier about that business with the table." Samuel makes a face and tries to defend Maher. The colonel gives him another hard stare and then, glancing at the white shirt Samuel's donned that day in his fanatical ambition to distinguish himself from the soldiers, he grumbles, gaze melting again, "Jolly nice shirt, that. But you don't match my troops, old chap, you don't match them at all!" And he bursts out in his famous laugh. That afternoon, it is Colonel Maher who confides in Samuel: "That Moore's a madman, an unpredictable maverick. But he's got backing. A childhood friend of John Baring's, he was. He can get away with doing whatever he bloody well wants. If Baring becomes prime minister in London one day, Moore'll be war secretary. Meanwhile, he struts about like an Oriental prince." Samuel listens without batting an eye. He'd like to ask where Moore gets the money for all this luxury in the middle of a country so poor and stripped bare, but he doesn't say a word, because he has no wish to hear Maher's petty replies.

One afternoon, they take a sharp turn and head back north to the gates of a town where Bellal was said to have been warmly welcomed a week ago. When the town is in sight, the colonel decides not to go in, and settles into an armchair in open country, under an acacia, like a king of old receiving surrender from the worthies of a besieged town. Around him, the officers and Samuel remain standing, and then from town come the worthies, in a group, alerted by their children and the local farmers. They bring gifts, which they lay on a rug at Moore's feet, and launch into muddled explanations about their relationship with Bellal and the fact that they've never been able to deny him what he wants, on pain of being slaughtered. "Powerful as all that, is he?" Moore asks, and the town's worthies, no doubt to justify their position, reply that he has hundreds of men, numbers three whole tribes among his followers, and has rifles. Before dismissing them, Moore reminds them that they haven't paid taxes for three years, and faced with their contrition, accepts the gifts in compensation for their unpaid taxes, then has these distributed among his troops before setting out again. "Well, don't look at me like that," he says to Samuel that evening. "Those gifts are worth less than what they owed, and for once, the soldiers are benefiting directly from taxes. Everyone's happy. Except you." Two days later, as they're nearing the mountains of Darfur and the lands of the Kababish, a caravan is reported to the west. Taking a small detachment that includes Samuel, the colonel hurries to meet it. They reach it at dusk, and it's like boarding an enemy ship: the horses draw up alongside the camels, pressing close against them; there are shouts, orders, black men running every which way, and then the convoy stops, its leader comes to see what the matter is. During the consultation, the colonel declares there have been persistent rumors to the effect that the slave trade has picked up again. Samuel doesn't know what to make of this strange excuse. The colonel alone is allowed to take a quick look at the few women in the convoy: three wives of a shopkeeper from Dongola traveling with their husband, and a nomad's daughter he'll marry up north. But no slaves. Meanwhile, night has fallen, swift as a stone. The rest of the regiment arrives, camp is made not far from the caravan, and as the night begins, the caravan's leader insists on inviting the colonel and his officers to dinner, a meal also shared with the merchants from Dongola. During the vigil, around a fire that seems to take part in every conversation with its crackle—shooting out little sparks, slinking flat as a sheepish dog, or coming back to life at a bundle of twigs fed it by a black man who never opens his mouth, there is talk of desert routes and the slave trade, and such a good time is had that the next morning everyone sets out to hunt gazelle together. They leave at an hour when the sky is soft, and throughout the morning, Moore's latest stylish rifles and the Sudanese's long-barreled guns with their mother-of-pearl stocks, mingle their joyous dins and bring seven gazelles to the dust, an almost miraculous number. That night, in camp, the animals are carved up and portioned out. Colonel Moore has the English troops served wine and date syrup from his own share of gifts received. The bivouac is transformed into a great gathering that with its songs, its fires where gazelle fat drips and drink flows copiously, comes to resemble an encampment of barbarian mercenaries.

That night, Samuel thinks to himself that it wouldn't take much for Colonel Moore's troops to turn, by slow degrees, into a column of irregulars imperceptibly outside the law, who would then set to scouring the lands they traveled, gradually going native and finally declaring their leader king of these realms. Just as these images are passing through his head, the colonel addresses him: "I know what you're thinking, Mister Ayyad. You're thinking that, instead of going to confront Bellal, I'm wasting my time with distractions worthy of a satrap. But can you tell me where to find this Bellal of yours? Besides, you're probably right to think what you're thinking—that I don't want to go fight him, because I'd crush him like a bug. And I don't want it to come to that. Have you read Slatin Pasha, Mister Ayyad? Yes? Then you must remember the Austrian's descriptions of the Mahdi's weapons, thousands of Negro soldiers with their white turbans, their rifles, and above them in the wind, thousands of banners. I've dreamed of such a sight for years. But since I've been in this country, all I've found is poverty, black men on mules, and preachers begging in the street. My secret hope, you see, is that Moussa Bellal finds me, with his Negro horsemen and his banners in the wind. But if that happens, do you think I'll want to fight him? Who wants to crush the stuff of his own dreams? Tell me that. You, perhaps? I hardly think so. So stop looking at me and judging me. We're made of the same stuff, you and I. I know it. I can read your thoughts, just as you read mine."

In the days that follow, the column resumes its brisk march, and none of the derelictions Samuel's dreamed about occur: beards don't go untrimmed, or shirts untucked, not a single turban makes an appearance among the British army uniforms, no banner unfurls over the men—everything remains impeccable and according to the strictest European discipline. Moore grows nervous, sometimes seeming to dodge any possible encounters with Bellal, and at other times seeking them out, making straight for watering holes or *zeribas* where he's been reported. But Bellal remains nowhere to be found, and after a week, the column enters the territory of Ali el Tom, chieftain of the powerful Kababish confederation. Colonel Moore's good spirits return, his eye starts its musical, mercurial back-and-forth, the idea of going to meet this powerful vassal of England fills him with jubilation. One morning, warriors appear, great fringed pennants flying over them. The scouts announce that these are the banners of Ali el Tom who has come in person to meet Colonel Moore, accompanied by several chieftains of subsidiary tribes. The meeting takes place at the foot of the rocky hills known as the Jebel Abu Asal. Ali el Tom is a young chieftain with a princely way about him and a dreamer's eyes. His skin is dark, but his features are more Arabian, and he knows a few words of English, which he uses to welcome Colonel Moore. The latter is delighted, and responds with the few words of Arabic he knows. Samuel and Maher can then intervene, and a conversation begins between Sheikh el Tom and the colonel as the two troops come in view of Sowdiri, a prosperous oasis surrounding hundreds of wells where

Ali el Tom holds court. Vast herds of camels watch the soldiers pass and by night, at the ochre-walled palace of Ali el Tom, in gardens of astounding baobabs, there is feasting and discussion atop low beds of sculpted wood. But news of Bellal is rare; he was recently spotted near Al Widan, then—nothing. Rumor has it that he has stirred up tribes near Taba. Colonel Moore listens, nods, then reaches out for a morsel of grilled lamb. Dozens of lambs are grilling over dozens of fires; the colonel is sitting to the right of Ali el Tom, who continues his explanations, speaking of Darfur as well as the principalities to the west where Bellal is beginning to worry local princes with his preaching and threats.

The next day, the two leaders are off to inspect the regions bordering the sultanate of Darfur. Although north of Um Badr, scouts report the presence of a sizeable Nihayat group near Jabal el Kadim. It is half a day's ride away on horseback, and Colonel Moore decides to go there. But on the way, during a break by a sycamore grove, a delegation of Nihayats is announced. It approaches, consisting of five imposing black men in *immas*, sparkling necklaces, and daggers on their belts. Speaking for their chief, they declare that Moussa Bellal has inadvertently strayed onto Kababish territory, that he has no hostile intentions, and that to prove it, he is inviting the colonel and Sheikh el Tom to dine with him that very day. Sitting in armchairs under the trees, Moore and el Tom deliberate, surrounded by their advisors. Ali el Tom is guarded about how to respond to this proposal, freighted with menace, but since Moore is in charge, they finally tell the delegation that they accept, and will attend.

*

The site of Moussa Bellal's banquet is on the fringe of an acacia wood, at the foot of a rocky hill known as the Shoulder of Beef. Assembled for it are Moore and his advisors, a few Kababish chieftains around el Tom, and Moussa Bellal's main warriors around their leader, who has enormous rings, a golden breastplate, and an unsettling gaze. They all gather at nightfall, because Moore and el Tom make their entrance only after a few reinforcements arrive from Sowdiri, a company that dismounts a stone's throw from where the banquet is being held. It is dark, then, when everything begins: the guests form a great circle. Massive bonfires that hurl nervous sparks toward the very stars light slaves slicing and serving mutton and grilled beef on giant platters, stuffed giraffe neck and monkey tongues browned in lamb fat.

"I wonder where you can have gotten all these ingredients," says el Tom to Moussa Bellal. "All these dishes lead one to believe you planned for this feast, that you didn't decide on the spur of the moment. I'm sure you're up to no good."

"You take us for impoverished Negroes, el Tom," Moussa Bellal replies. "And now you're simply finding out that isn't the case. But rest assured," he adds with a laugh, "I am no Muhammad Ali."

As Moussa Bellal has directed this allusion to the banquet during which the Egyptian viceroy exterminated all the generals in his army at Colonel Moore, the latter, seated on a saffron rug, declares, to lighten the mood, that there are worse crimes than Muhammad Ali's, and launches into the tale of how Atreus threw his own brother a lavish banquet whose dishes were made from the flesh of his nephews, cooked in the most extravagant sauces. Exclamations of horror and curses ring out from the pagans at the same time as Bellal's laughter, which Moore contemplates with amusement, satisfied with the effect his story has had. After which, Captain Covington recounts the dinner the fox served the stork, and the one the stork served in return. The decidedly very cultured Sheikh el Tom remarks that the tale is one taken from the fables of Ibn al-Muqaffa', which Covington refutes, alleging it is by the Frenchman La Fontaine (which he pronounces La Fantayne). Moussa Bellal, apparently bored by literary debates or finding the whole business has gotten out of hand, turns to Samuel then—he has not taken his eye off him since Moore's troops arrived, seeming to wonder just who this civilian (for Samuel wears a hat and tunic) can be, looking British as he does but speaking Arabic, a very smooth Arabic, not Egyptian Arabic, much less the effeminate or falsely virile Arabic of British translators. So he turns to Samuel and asks him if he, too, has a story about a banquet. Samuel tells the one about the youngest, somewhat disdained son of a rich Beiruti family whom cousins from the elder branch of the family invite to dinner one night, offering him a miserly meal with neither variety nor the slightest display of pomp common to their house. The young cousin is cruelly offended, but by chance he hears about the famous French illusionist who is now the talk of the town's high society. He then decides to extend an invitation to his cousins in return. When the night comes, the cousins are pleasantly surprised to find the illusionist himself among the guests. None of them realize he is there not as a guest, but to ply his trade for a tidy sum. All throughout dinner, the ladies with their stylish hair, the self-important gentlemen, and the young, stuck-up daughters from the family's elder branch ask him loudly and laughingly about his powers, not for a moment suspecting that the sumptuous meal of stuffed lamb, cooked calf's brains, and as many sweets as an Oriental imagination might conjure is in fact but an illusion, and they are spending their evening, under the quietly ironic gaze of their host, the cousin scorned, eating bluster from empty dishes and delightedly relishing puffs of nothing from platters laden with thin air.

When Samuel is done, Moussa Bellal lets out a great roar of laughter, and then, just as gazelle tripe stuffed with pigeon hearts is being served, he declares to Colonel Moore with delectation, "Don't worry, I haven't had your nephews roasted. Everything you're eating is halal, and I guarantee you that it's good meat from actual animals, butchered and served up by my slaves—actual slaves, too (and here, he seems to take pleasure from insisting on the subject of slaves, for slavery is banned in Sudan, and faced with this insistence which is itself a provocation, no one bats an eye, because Moore doesn't say a word), actual slaves," Moussa Bellal goes on with jubilation, "all wearing what slaves always have and always will."

Then, falling silent, he gives a wave of his hand. A slight, imperceptible swell rolls through the ranks of his warriors and their chieftains. A brief glimmer of worry shows in Moore's eye, but the colonel remains still, sitting cross-legged, left hand on his knee. Ali el Tom exchanges a furtive glance with one of his relatives; meanwhile, Samuel is still wondering about Moussa Bellal's insistence on what slaves wear. Then a cry rings out: Captain Covington, letting out a swear, has just gotten to his feet, one hand on his revolver holster, even as Colonel Maher holds him back by his pants leg. Ali el Tom remains still as stone. Moore, who hasn't moved either, has a pout on his face that might be mistaken for a smile; the other officers seem paralyzed by what's going on, or their leader's icy immobility, and what everyone has just discovered, Samuel finally sees, though he's been staring at it for several long seconds: the sudden appearance of dozens of slaves, bearing on their shoulders a new batch of spits or large platters of meat, and all identically clad, as in some burlesque spectacle, barefoot but with regulation caps, in the green dress uniform blazoned with the Order of the Garter of officers of the British Empire.

The chase begins half an hour later, in the middle of the night, just enough time for Moore and his companions to rejoin the reinforcements, on the alert all this time. The utter darkness makes things difficult. The site of the feast, where fires still burn, is soon occupied, but nothing remains save leftovers of outlandish victuals and dozens of sheep and oxen ready for roasting, soon to be the occasion of another feast, one for vultures and hyenas. Two hour later, the first group of Moussa Bellal's warriors and slaves are caught by surprise in a pass between two rocky hills. Once they are captured, the hunt must stop, for the darkness is thick and the thousand stars that bring sky and earth closer together cannot make up for the glow of an absent moon. Only a few scouts of Ali el Tom's venture on ahead. They return at first light. Thanks to them, the armies are soon on Bellal's heels. As soon as the chase resumes, Colonel Moore, galloping beside Samuel, keeps grumbling about how he can't believe what that man did, he just can't believe it. By the time day has fully dawned, they are encroaching on the borders of the Sultanate of Darfur, riding full speed through a savannah of rolling hills dotted with acacia groves, when suddenly Moussa's warriors come into view. They are quickly surrounded and surrender without a fight. Moussa has gone on ahead, they explain.

Ali el Tom awaits a signal from Moore, who nods, and the chase goes on, British soldiers and Kababish warriors together. A bit later, it is a whole tribe, with its women and slaves, that is caught unawares, surrounded and stopped on the spot. Moussa Bellal has evidently left everything behind. All that was once his is now in the hands of Moore and Ali el Tom.

At dawn the next morning, Moore decides that the hunt cannot continue. Although nominally under English supervision, the mountains of Darfur are still free; press on and the risk of sparking off hostilities with Sultan Ali Dinar becomes too great. A council is held under three tamarind trees. Rough maps of the region are spread out on folding tables. A dry wind flips their edges back or sends them flying. Moore rises, declaring there's nothing left to be done. Ali el Tom says Bellal will likely seek refuge in the sultanates of the west, where he is from. Moore announces that at any rate, England will not intervene in the west, it's too close to the zone of French influence, and he's not about to risk war with the French over a few Mahdists. And he brings the meeting to a close. But as the troops prepare to turn back, the colonel draws Samuel aside and Samuel takes this chance to tell him what he thinks—that is, if they had gone on, they could've had Bellal, and Ali Dinar would've been glad to have him out of the way.

"I know," answers Moore. "But I didn't want to crush him like a bug, when he had neither men nor weapons."

Samuel observes that Bellal is now out of reach. Not at all, Moore asserts, and someone will have to go out there and finish the job, with support from the sultans of the west, who hate him.

"But he'll have rebuilt his forces in the meantime," Samuel protests.

"So much the better," says Moore. "This way we'll give him a chance at a truly royal defeat."

"I'll wager I'm the one you want for this job," says Samuel.

"I'd gladly go myself," says the colonel. "You know that. But I can't abandon my men. And you're the one I'm appointing. Don't do anything I wouldn't do."

"But what guarantee do we have that the sultans of the west will agree to go and fight Bellal?" Samuel persists.

"I've told you already. They hate him," Moore replies. "All you have to do is negotiate cleverly with them and be persuasive. Just think—if you pull it off, you may be lucky enough to be the last to look upon the splendors of the ancient world."

✳

Samuel leaves. He crosses the Marrah Mountains despite Sultan Ali Dinar's standing death threat against any White Man who dares set foot there. Accompanying him is a Sudanese aide-de-camp, a native of Darfur we shall call Gawad. Samuel wears an imma round his neck at all times, above his shirt collar, which he rolls up over his face to hide the color of his skin in cause of any run-ins with the wrong sort. But the two men meet no one, or almost no one—perhaps, in the distance, a slow procession of peasants, donkeys, and oxen dragging their feet in strange silence, or perhaps, in the setting sun that spreads infinite gold across the savannah, a cortege of women, children, and mules, a diaphanous apparition. Perhaps one morning they even near, without noticing, a dozen huts, down to one side; it is the palaver of two farmers standing in the middle of the only path through the village that draws their attention, and with nudges and hands placed over their mouths they warn each other to be wary. But each time, they pass by unseen, and one morning the savannah of the west appears, with the vast yellow steppe of Dar Safa, stippled with acacias, on the horizon. But they still have to find a way down from the plateau, for the available paths are always clogged with small caravans or families returning to the heights. Moving northward, straying from the straightest course, they finally find a way down and reach the plain. A few days later, Qasim Wad Jabr, the Sultan of Safa, agrees to lend his assistance to bring down Moussa Bellal. But he has conditions. Seated on the doorstep to his house, amidst the buzz of insects and the cries of women debating beside large earthenware jars a few yards away, he tells Samuel that nothing is ever free: if England wishes to defeat its enemies, it must be generous with its friends.

Samuel listens, sitting on a wooden stool. His hair is no doubt disheveled, and he cannot look away from the sultan's mother, an enormous queen who nods off during the meeting while being fanned by huge ostrich plumes. And as he listens, Samuel realizes that the generosity the sultan is asking from the English must above all allow him to impose his suzerainty over the other Safawi chieftains, to force them to join a confederation of which he shall be the uncontested leader. That very night, leaning against a massive acacia, Samuel writes a letter to Colonel Moore. He asks for guns on behalf of the Sultan of Safa, rifles and pistols in great quantities, and as quickly as possible. Then he sends Gawad off with the letter, not really knowing what to hope for. Meanwhile, he spends his days at the sultan's court, playing knucklebone with Qasim Wad Jabr, discussing military strategy over maps drawn in the sand with sticks, and learning the Safawi language. And no doubt he explains to Wad Jabr, during a stop on one of the hunting trips where they kill gazelles with javelins or single-shot rifles, that there's no guarantee he'll get weapons. "Then Bellal will not be brought down," the sultan distractedly replies.

One night, during a meal in honor of the chieftains of tribes allied to the sultan, in front of Wad Jabr's dwelling, which the fire makes look like a colossal palace, the conversations revolve around Samuel's person, what brought him to Darfur, and the few Lebanese known to have been in the region. A Safawi chief tells the story of a Syro-Lebanese slave trader who worked for Sultan Rabih of Borno. Qasim Wad Jabr tells the one about the Lebanese man who left with Emin Pasha for Equatoria, thinking to start a trade in precious woods, only to die of dysentery by the old hero's side. After which, it is Samuel who tells a story, one he heard at the Syrian Protestant College, from that fellow countryman who set about running guns to various Abysinnian kings, in collaboration with a French adventurer who had apparently been a poet in his own land. One day, as he was escorting a load of rifles for the Negus, he was captured by the latter's enemies, who decided to execute him on the spot with the very weapons he was readying to deliver. And as trays filled with morsels of beef pass from one guest to the next, Samuel taking some in turn, he goes on, to the amused and shining eyes of the chieftains and their retinues, to tell that the rifles refused to kill the arms dealer, that the execution squad fired its salvo at the condemned man lashed to a tree, but not a single bullet touched him. The Abysinnians cried out that it was a miracle, loosed the man's bonds, and let him go. The audience laughs and waits for an explanation, platters of meat making another round, and Samuel clarifies that the execution took place on a highly magnetized patch of land, and quite likely, lodestone in the ground caused the bullets to veer off course—that was one possible explanation; there were others, including a miracle itself, and now his audience is murmuring admiringly and invoking God, in whom the only true knowledge resides. After which a singular silence falls and Samuel notices that, in the gilded orange light where shadows play to and fro at the will of the flames, his story, which links a Lebanese man, guns, and a miracle, is giving rise to strange reveries in the heads and gazes around him. He grows worried at this, because at first he himself believed only very moderately in this business of guns, and now he wonders anxiously how the sultan's disappointment will manifest itself toward him if promises are not kept. But they are. The guns arrive, an entire arsenal transported by an endless caravan descending from the north after skirting the Marrah Mountains. From the summit of a small ridge, Wad Jabr's troops come to a halt beneath banners green and white, admire the hundreds of camels unreeling in a placid line across the desert. A few hours later, Gawad hands Samuel a letter from the colonel concerning guns and also gold. Samuel looks up from the letter and his eyes meet Gawad's. From the man's look, Samuel understands the gold is there, whole bags of it, that it would be best kept discreetly from the reach of greedy hands.

*

In the weeks that follow, Wad Jabr unites all the tribes that are loyal to him. A wind of power and bellicose intent sweeps through the region. Dark legions arrive from the west and the north, warriors with heads wrapped in turbans with a thousand folds. Princes, rare of name, fierce of eye, and thunderous of voice, come to meet them under venerable nettle trees. Wad Jabr's camp swells like a stormy sea, and banners flash from every corner. "All this is thanks to you," the sultan tells Samuel one morning, but Samuel remains silent, for it is Moore's madness, his gold and his rifles, that have fanned this sumptuous inferno, that have made possible this theatre whose stage manager and sole spectator Samuel now is. One morning, emissaries from Moussa Bellal arrive, bringing Wad Jabr comminatory orders to surrender to the will of the Almighty, as the Mad Mahdi has done, and rid himself of this Christian envoy, or else war will be inevitable. Wad Jabr burns the letter in a fire over which kid lambs are roasting, and the battle finally comes to pass, near a place known as the King's Well. Banners by the hundreds fly in the wind, blazing in the heavens, raging with their thousand colors, their Koranic verses flinging out imprecations. Beneath them, black horsemen by the thousands, silent and magnificent, face one another in two snaking lines in the middle of the desert. At the heart of the opposing ranks, a fringed green and black banner signals the unsettling presence of Moussa Bellal. That madman Moore was right, thinks Samuel, it really is spectacular. But ten minutes later, he forgets its beauty, the fusillade is violent, the roar and the charge are horrifying, and there is he is, in his European suit, an imma around his head, dragged thoughtlessly into slaughter, instinctively flailing to save his skin, firing his revolver point-blank, then tossing it away and brandishing a saber as if he'd done this kind of thing all his life, desperately whirling it around himself, and blood is splattering his face, dark hands are flying all around him, still gripping their sabers, dark throats suddenly adorned with red necklaces and convulsed eyes. After which, when Moussa Bellal's troops have been decimated, and there is nothing left of Moussa himself but a head on a pike, Samuel thinks that, too, would please Moore, it's very Orientalist, and he snickers, a horribly nervous snicker, realizing he's shaking like a leaf, and keeps shaking as the Sultan laughs his vast laugh, his teeth whiter than jasmine.

4

AMONG THE MANY STORIES OF THOSE MEN WHO, FEELING hemmed in by the mountains and the sea, left Lebanon in the early twentieth century, the story of Shafik Abyad is without a doubt one of the most singular. And yet it began somewhat unassumingly, when this carpenter's son from the village of Beit Chabab, in the Lebanese mountains, left for Egypt in the first decade of the new century. According to firsthand accounts I was able to obtain from that era, it seems he first alighted in Alexandria, where he found work with an Italian carpenter or cabinetmaker who supplied doors, windows, and sculpted woodwork for the villas and modern apartment buildings with which the city was just beginning to bedeck itself. Another of Abyad's tasks for his employer was to seek out precious fittings and fixtures from the abandoned monuments in the Arab old town. Bourgeois Greeks, Lebanese, and Jews sometimes integrated these elements into modern ensembles when commissioning residences where art nouveau rubbed shoulders with repurposings and Oriental references. But Shafik Abyad likely also ended up supplying antiques to Western dealers, for whom he became a well-known broker, buying from or helping himself to ruined edifices of Arabian Alexandria, which he would explore on his own before bringing in first local artisans to remove roof beams, ceilings, or *mashrabiyas*, and then mule drivers to transport these to a depot in the Mansheya district. All this must have allowed him to set aside quite a tidy sum, and one day, in some unaccountable fashion—though doubtless with a view to diversifying his territory and sources, or maybe on the advice of his former Italian employer— here he is, leaving for Libya.

In Tripoli, he finds lodgings with the small Italian community, and in a city that is still an overgrown village of filthy, reeking alleys, he resumes his explorations. Since he speaks Arabic, locals receive him without complaint, despite his European suit, his too-thin neck aswim in a starched collar, his mustachio à la Léon Blum. That's the kind of man he was, this Shafik Abyad, whose life would become intimately entwined with my grandfather's for years: skinny, with a gaunt face, bushy mustache, and hollow cheeks. Despite a slight air of grumpiness about him, shopkeepers and artisans help him in his search; he finds a few pieces he then sends on to Alexandria by boat. All this goes on for, say, a year or so, until one day he spots a small Arabian palace in the neighborhood by the citadel. It has a few handsome doors, finely-worked windows, a Moorish marble pool, a small mashrabiya, and two carved stone chimneys like fat pointed bells, as well as a wall painted with birds and fountains, a decorative ceiling and staircase, and even four large mirrors in bronze frames, survivors of a time when the spoils of piracy furnished the town's markets. Its owner, a wholesaler of dates and dried fruits in a white burnous and Oriental slippers, takes him on a tour of the edifice, now a home to local hens and goats. When, stepping over a fallen roof beam, Abyad asks the wholesaler how much he wants for the woodwork, doors, ceiling, and mirrors, the man thinks for a moment; he has a string of amber prayer beads and a somewhat sly air about him. He mutters figures under his breath and then, like a man who for the rock-bottom price of a pound will let you walk off with every orange he has, verging as they are on rot, he offers to let Abyad have the entire building for the price of the woodwork and the mirrors.

Although these proceedings might, in their details, seem less than trustworthy, this much is beyond doubt: one fine day, Shafik Abyad indeed finds himself the owner of a little gem in the labyrinth of Tripoli's Arab quarter. Careful not to spoil the integrity of the whole, he leaves the woodwork and the mirrors where they are, but soon realizes he has an unsalable property on his hands. Perhaps he considers having it restored and renting it out to a consulate, but he soon gives up on that and another plan, absolutely unhinged, comes to mind. I do not know—nor will anyone, ever—what planted the seed of that incredible idea in his mind. He may have heard tell of those desert nations where princes build their houses just as peasants do, from baked clay or brick, and thought a stone palace with frescoed walls, delivered to their doorstep, would dazzle them. Unless it was some camel-driver who told him that the kings of these lands, now vassals of France, were beginning to have abodes built for themselves in order to show European colonists that the ancient traditions of Islam and Arabs were in no way inferior to theirs. The fact remains that one morning, Shafik Abyad organizes the dismantling of his little seraglio stone by stone. After which he charters an enormous caravan that he loads up with every last piece: frescoed walls, mirrors, chimneys, pool adorned in Moorish style, finely wrought roof cut into three sections, carefully detached staircase. Then he enters into endless discussions and negotiations with the caravaners on which way to go and the agreed-on prices that grow and change from one day to the next, and finally the convoy carrying the Arab palace in pieces leaves Tripoli for parts south.

The initial destination is likely the region around Lake Chad. The trip takes five weeks, with the usual difficulties: endless, incomprehensible stops at oases, inexplicable sulking from the guides when Abyad lets his irritation show, nerves due to rumors of plunderers nearby, the truth of which Shafik doubts. But nonetheless they press on, they cross the Libyan desert, the Fezzan with its rare oases, then the Tibesti with its mountains like masterpieces wrought by Titans. For a week, mustache drooping, collar starched, and eyes wide before these colossal natural sculptures, Shafik Abyad must look like a pioneer of the American West passing beneath cliffs in the Nevadan desert, except that his caravan consists not of squeaking carts but slow ruminants with an air of superiority, hauling not the meager effects of wretched migrants but a miniature palace with arabesque motifs on its doors and frescoed walls, brought all this way to be sold to black princes still somewhat hypothetical, it's true, but to whom the praises of this singular product will soon be sung.

*

And yet of course, a palace cannot be sold like a crate of fruit. In Borno, Abyad unpacks the thousand pieces of his princely abode before the local sultan's, with its towers and adobe walls. Beneath great perfumed canopies, the sultan, with his court in tow, comes to look it over like a customer and his family strolling absent-mindedly among the scattered wares of an opulent flea market. At last, his eye settles upon one of the bronze Italian mirrors and the decorative ceiling. "All or nothing," Abyad replies, then packs it all back up and sets out again. In Kanem, to the east, where since the recent French conquest there has no longer been a sultanate, but only powerful chieftains, he drops anchor several times in the middle of market towns, on squares of red sand surrounded by earthen dwellings whose walls and clay towers his caravaners sneer at, as if they themselves were now guardians of the beauty they've hauled across the desert and defended from plunderers. They must wait each time, for the princes are hesitant; they come to see the item for sale or send along dignitaries in slippers who strut about, chest disdainfully outthrust. There is endless nattering; Shafik Abyad sketches out the plans, relates the number of rooms and the height of the ceilings, and he is made to wait. He waits for days and weeks in nameless corners of the savannah that, every morning, become marketplaces, mats laid out on the ground. Babbling women in garish dresses squabble over the price of grasses and roots and sheep or veal carcasses, while lengthy herds of living bovines and ovines belonging to local worthies keep wandering in and out of the tall mud-and-straw houses, passing between fragments of the palace transported from Tripoli, or originally sometimes even Rome or Damascus, which seem like the fruits of fabulous plunder that pirates have strewn across a beach, the better to divvy up. Then come the nights, and there is nothing but lonely trees and red sand. Great sheets are laid over the royal rubble of Shafik Abyad, and the fires lit all around make them look like an army of ghosts.

After a few months, the caravan leader demands dues for every day of waiting. It will be the ruin of him, but Abyad pays, though the black princes never want the palace. It's too expensive for them; they're like petits bourgeois in whose home some addled salesman has just shown a hundred-carat diamond once worn by the Queen of England; they try to negotiate, they want it all except the north wing, or just the divan and the stateroom, or only the ceiling, or the wall with the birds on it, or the mirrors—always the mirrors!—and Abyad says no, all or nothing, and goes on his way again. After a year, he's changed camels and camel drivers three times and is seriously starting to fear raiders, for word of him has spread about. What's more, the nomad tribes he meets want to see the merchandise; tales of a castle straight from the Arabian nights roaming their inhospitable lands have fired their imaginations. Abyad balks but, fearing their touchiness, pulls back the sheet covering one of the mirrors pressed flat to a camel's flank. The silvering, which has reflected the figures of Roman and Sicilian princesses, and then Barbary corsairs or their favorite Circassian women, now shows nomad chieftains with cream-puff turbans and wispy beards their own images, a spectacle at which they sometimes laugh and sometimes meet with an offended pout, staring aggressively at the vast halted convoy carrying, beneath canvas tarps, its staterooms, divans, and staircases of sculpted wood. At every such encounter, Abyad fears the worst. At last, at a fort held by the French army and commanded by a lieutenant from Dijon, he requests an escort. The lieutenant, who can't yet bring himself to believe what Abyad has told him about his cargo, wants to see it for himself. Upon discovering the great hewn blocks, the ornate pool, the carved ceilings supported by equines that look like snooty ladies, he lets out a fantastic burst of laughter and declares that he's just understood the etymology of the word "caravanserai": a seraglio on a caravan! So that's it, eh? and laughs till there are tears in his eyes, his noncommissioned officers looking amusedly on and the black soldiers unruffled. Shafik Abyad, who spent a few years at a French Marist Brothers school in the Lebanese mountains, no doubt understands the wordplay, but doesn't laugh. He's more emaciated than ever, his ascot looks like a tired old hanky, his shirt floats about his skeletal frame, his suspenders hang askew, and he's starting to look lost, for his eyes are too wide for a face that shrinks a little more each day.

*

Of course, the French lieutenant cannot spare him an escort, and so Shafik Abyad comes to an astonishing decision. He decides to leave a part of his property in the zeriba, under the minuscule garrison's guard—the east wing, let us say (though in fact, we cannot speak of wings east or west, it's all jumbled up now, and everything will depend on where it's reassembled), along with the mashrabiya, the doors, and one of the bell-shaped chimneys, not to mention a good many numbered stone blocks. With the west wing, including among other things the massive Italian mirrors with their bronze frames, the other chimney, and the frescoed wall, he sets out once more in search of a buyer, a new African king or powerful tribal chieftain anxious to treat himself to a palatial little gift.

He heads south, and on the way doubtless believes luck is smiling on him at last, for he learns that the sultan of the Masalit has just been overthrown by one of his cousins. New ruler, new seraglio, Abyad is probably thinking, but before he reaches his destination, a messenger tells him that because of the situation in Dar Massalit, the zeriba has had to be abandoned for another farther south. Leaving the caravan by a well, he turns back and, four days later, finds his merchandise intact in the desert fort but left to the four winds and all the sands of the savannah. He spends a night amidst the disorder of this packed-up, portable construction site. Eyes riveted to the twinkling stars, he wonders for the first time if he hasn't made a colossal mistake in leaving Tripoli with this cumbersome cargo. A few days later, he rejoins the rest of his party to learn, stoically, that there's been a quarrel among its members, that some of them have decided to leave, taking the staircase, a section of the elaborate roof, and one large mirror with them for their pains. The west wing is maimed, though its stones, all those numbered stones, are still there. But who will want so many stones, even if they are numbered? Nevertheless, Shafik Abyad continues on his way. He no longer wants to go to Masalit. He wishes to stay in the French-controlled areas, in order to recover what he left in the fort as fast as he can. He's not even looking for a buyer anymore, not a king nor an African chieftain nor a Bedouin. He wanders and goes in circles awhile, hoping to find some camels to buy along the way. And that is when, one and a half years after leaving Tripoli, two hundred and fifty miles south of the Sultanate of Ouaddaï and one hundred eighty miles west of Darfur, as he is dining beside a fire one night with members of a tribe he met by a well, he hears tell for the first time of a Lebanese man fighting beside the sultan of Safa and at last, from down in that chasm where he seems to have touched rock bottom, he glimpses a glimmer of hope.

*

For while he, Shafik Abyad, has been wandering the deserts of Chad, Samuel Ayyad is still with Qasim Wad Jabr. In the wake of Moussa Bellal's defeat, Samuel is helping him rebuild the former Sultanate of Safa, the last black kingdom in the region. And so he finds himself mixed up in tribal warfare, struggles between chieftains; he witnesses great bloodstained banners, surrenders under the baobabs, and severed heads. Moore's gold sometimes serves to negotiate a matrimonial alliance, or to buy spies. But for all the rest, the rifles are enough, and long talks by firelight or on sofas in the shade of acacias, in the dry desert wind. Besides, in Wad Jabr's eyes, Samuel is worth more than the gold whose burdensome custody he's been entrusted with, gold Gawad transports in little bags whose contents no one suspects. His mere presence stands surety, for Samuel passes for an envoy from Khartoum, Cairo, even London; everyone takes him for the man tasked with implementing English policy in the region, and when he speaks, they all listen in silence, as if John Baring, the powerful English consul in Cairo, or even the British prime minister spoke through him. We might go so far as to imagine the presence in that region of the man who will one day be my grandfather makes France believe the British have decided to intervene in western Darfur, a fact that drives them, in 1912, to lay their own hands on the neighboring Sultanate of Ouaddaï. Samuel lets them think what they will, and inside, laughs when he thinks that he's there only due to the whims of a slightly batty colonel. And sometimes, he, too, has his doubts; Moore suddenly seems to him a dreadful manipulator. But he doesn't care, he himself might even be filled with the colonel's dreams now, and during this entire time, which is to say, six months, or a year, or two—at any rate, the time it takes Shafik Abyad to get close enough to this part of the Sudan, with his woolgathering little seraglio on the backs of hundreds of camels like the flotsam of a splendid ship bobbing on the waves after a storm—during all this time, Samuel has been dashing through the desert beneath great banners, in a European suit, an imma on his head, his light skin bronzed by the sun, stiffened by wind and sand, his gaze still like a prow, sailing ahead of the world. They call him, with fearful respect, El Inglizi, or El Lebnani, but the sultan calls him Samouyil Wad Nassib, Samuel son of Nassib, after his father, the literature professor from the Lebanese mountains, and whenever the sultan calls Samuel this, in front of other chieftains or by firelight vigil, he tells him that you Lebanese are incredible, you mingle Christian and Muslim names so well that I can't tell anymore if you're one or the other—so you, Samouyil, what are you, eh? What are you? And Samuel mumbles that he is both at once—and that, Wad Jabr, you will never understand, no matter how many times I explain, you will never understand. And it is no doubt by addressing him respectfully as Samouyil Wad Nassib one morning that a famished black man flanked by two turbaned warriors from the sultan's guard appears before him and hands him a letter. Let us say this happens in the heart of an oasis, by a well where the horses are giving themselves a good shake. Great birds rise into the dazzling sky above the acacias and the broom. Samuel, sitting on a rug, back against a tree trunk and feet on a crate, sits up uncomprehendingly, hair disheveled, eyes cheerful, and adopts an expression of curiosity that makes him squint, opens the letter, and learns of the existence of Shafik Abyad.

5

WHEN TWO LEBANESE EMIGRANTS MEET EACH OTHER thousands of miles from their native land, the first thing they do, I suppose, is delight in greeting each other in their common tongue, rediscovering those familiar liquid syllables, those open vowels, savoring that easing of elocutional effort, especially if, as is no doubt the case with Samuel Ayyad and Shafik Abyad, they've spent years speaking a rough, abrupt Arabic not their own. Here they are shaking hands, a bit like Stanley upon finding Emin Pasha or Livingstone, and Samuel is probably saying something like "Shafik Abyad, I presume," but in the Beiruti tongue. Shafik Abyad nods, holding on to the man's hand for a spell, the man who's just joined Shafik where Shafik has stopped to wait for him, a few hours on foot from the abandoned city of Ouara, amidst lightly wooded hills covered in broom and even holm oaks not entirely unreminiscent of Lebanon. And this is one of the first things Samuel remarks on to Shafik. The latter agrees, and as they go to sit in the shade of an acacia, on rugs or low chairs, the two future accomplices recall the pines of Chouf and the olive trees of Koura, then speak of their origins, trying to untangle their genealogies, unreel the itineraries of their lives to see if, somewhere, they might not have crossed paths, or if an unsuspected family tie connects them, for Lebanon is so small. Sipping tea that the caravaners sitting off to one side serve them (to another side sit Gawad and Samuel's escort of riders), they finally come to what has brought them to this thankless land.

When Shafik is done with his story, he takes Samuel for a stroll among the hundreds of bundles of freight spread out beneath the sycamores, among the shrubs of broom and the thorny thickets, lavish yet pathetic, like a royal eviction overseen by a bailiff. And that is when Samuel discovers the mirrors in their bronze frames beneath their worn tarps, the wall frescoed with birds tossed on the sand like an old rug in the sun's harsh menace, and the fragments of sculpted ceiling, one side concealed by coverings of makeshift scraps and the other peeking through, like bedmates disputing a single too-small blanket. Now as Shafik drags him around with a tired air from one piece to another of his Barbary palace pathetically unbundled in the middle of the savannah, Samuel stares hard at his fellow countryman, whose explanations he no longer hears. Besides, these grow ever shorter and wearier, finally no more than vague hand waves that serve as much to point out the numbered sections of a Moorish marble fountain or a bell-shaped chimney as to say that all this is most likely destined for imminent disaster, and sooner or later, Samuel naturally comes to wonder if Shafik Abyad isn't a bit touched in the head. Then he thinks if maybe, after suffering the whims of Colonel Moore, he must now suffer those of Shafik Abyad. But he is the kind of man to shoulder other people's whims, to make them his own, and here he is letting himself be swept along on Shafik's oddball odyssey. At first, it is just to lend a helping hand, of course—Samuel has twenty-five black warriors (from Gawad's tribe, on loan from Qasim Wad Jabr, but who would let themselves be torn to shreds for him), he has maps (which are useless, since he's the one who draws them up from what he sees, but they give him confidence), and above all he has Moore's gold (of which he says not a word, at first). And besides, things are always easier with two people.

So at first, the two men decide to recover what was left behind in the French zeriba. It is Samuel who goes to the small fort, where it is clear tribes have camped and caravans stopped for the night. There are traces of fire, the fragments stored there have been rummaged through, but on the whole they appear present and accounted for, from the mashrabiya to the carved doors and the bell-shaped chimney. From all appearances, the tribal chieftains and camel-drivers must have scratched their heads over the spectacle of this treasure straight out of Ali Baba's cavern; they must have looked in vain for gold or precious objects, for lack of which they contented themselves with sleeping amidst this incomprehensible pomp before departing with a shrug of their shoulders.

When the east wing has been reunited with the rest of the palace, the latter, more or less intact, sets out once more on the backs of a hundred animals, under the protection of twenty-five warriors and the double command of Shafik Abyad and Samuel Ayyad. For months, they will pay visits once more to tribal chieftains and black princes, in a vast procession it takes ten minutes at a gallop to travel from one end to the other, stretching out against the same unchanging backdrop of red sand, dotted by thickets of broom, acacia, and baobab, where, from time to time, the wind raises pillars of dust that seem to bend and beckon to travelers. But the convoy's grandeur in fact conceals massive problems. Shafik Abyad is bankrupt, he owes his men money, they follow him now only in hopes of getting their due. Meanwhile, they do as they please, give their opinion on each new destination instead of serving as guides or looking after the animals, balk at going one place, believing another will be luckier, as if selling the cargo had become their business and no longer that of the two Lebanese men—and this is an excuse for endless consultations, discussions, and disputes from which Shafik Abyad emerges exhausted and demoralized. And so it is that after a fortnight of this carrying-on, Samuel intervenes, brandishing the gold from the British Treasury chest, which Colonel Moore has placed at his disposal for other causes, and right before Shafik Abyad's astonished eyes, he convenes the escort and pays them what they're owed. To lend the ceremony some decorum and make an impression, he sits himself down like a king beneath a baobab, has himself surrounded by his black warriors, and it is Gawad who, on his orders, settles everyone's debts. After which he declares in a tone that brooks no rejoinder that from now on the two White Men will decide everything without discussion. Then, turning to Shafik, who feigns protest, he explains in an aside that this money was but a loan on his part, and he expects to be reimbursed once the palace is sold.

✳

Now of course, the palace remains unsalable. The lands they pass through are ever poorer, their princes ever less powerful. The sultan of Tama sends messengers to hasten the caravan along, claiming interest, but when it arrives before his brick dwelling he recants, no doubt finding the merchandise above his means, and so as not to lose face, he declares himself indisposed for several days. In Sila, the sultan receives Samuel and Shafik, but gives them a disillusioned speech: "I have the French to the west and the English to the east. In due course, one or the other will send in their armies, and perhaps one day soon there will be no more sultan of Sila, so what is the point of purchasing a new domicile to house a dynasty without a future?" Then he falls silent, and the next day, the caravan heads out again. One afternoon, a few of Samuel's riders go off game hunting. They take their time, vanishing from view, but from atop a small hill, come in sight again in the savannah, and Samuel, to entertain his troops a little, has one of the bronze-framed mirrors uncovered, using it to reflect sunlight and send signals to the lost horsemen. Then Shafik Abyad, who has recovered his good mood thanks to Samuel's presence beside him, laughingly suggests that instead of selling their cargo, they could use the stones and mirrors to build a lighthouse meant for men and beasts lost in the desert. Everyone thinks this a marvelous idea, and much more useful than a palace no one wants. Meanwhile, every morning, Shafik and Samuel use the mirrors to perform their daily grooming, unswaddling the great cheval glasses with their frames of twined acanthus leaves, before which they shave themselves and scrub their bodies. As a result of their meeting, the two men feel a sudden need for some of the creature comforts they've been deprived of for years. They dream of a cigar after every meal, and also sitting down at a table to eat. For this last, they commit the sacrilege of setting two carved wooden doors atop a chest inlaid with mother-of-pearl, thus fashioning the furniture of their dreams. And then one day, on their way through a French fort, they spend a fortune on a captain's common office chairs (and faced with the sovereign stamped with King George's likeness that Samuel displays, the French officer hesitates, then pockets the coin, declaring, "Ah! You're British Army, then. I guess they're rich in the British Army!"). After which, having lugged a seraglio and its furnishings around for months, even years—its bronzes, woodwork, and frescoed walls museums the world over would envy—they sit down with childish glee, they sit down each night at a table on a pair of rickety chairs in the middle of the desert, or among the acacias of an oasis, or beneath a baobab in the middle of nowhere, surrounded by animals that have been unloaded and a camp that has been pitched, conversing over dinner as they might in the dining room of a middle class Beiruti household.

But apart from that, nothing changes. Upon leaving the sultan of Sila, Shafik declares unsmilingly that he's had enough, he doesn't believe in it anymore, he might just go to Khartoum to try and sell off the most interesting pieces of his merchandise, pity about the rest. Just then, Samuel thinks of the sultan of Safa, but Safa is far to the south now, and he doesn't want to go back there anymore. His mission is over, and he realizes that he, too, dreams of returning to Khartoum. To be done with this business once and for all, he suggests heading westward once more, toward Ouaddaï: "Let's try one last time. I hear Ouaddaï princes are richer than the others, and if it doesn't work, we'll head back to Khartoum." Shafik Abyad lets himself be won over; they set course westward, and all this will still take months upon months on foot accompanied by the unrelenting routine of the desert and the savannahs, arguments among the caravaners; camels that throw incredible tantrums, tearing out eyes and biting off ears, scorpions in shoes and snakes in blankets, days so hot the caravan can get going only in late afternoon, freezing nights when they sleep with their heads against the animals' haunches; but also iridescent nights when they lie down with a constellation to their left, and when they wake a bit later, there it is on the right; brief and bloody hunts for gazelles, panthers, and lions everyone fantasizes about but no one ever sees; and erratic tribes, distant caravans, wells where suddenly a crowd crops up as at a fountain in a city, umbrella-like acacias and imposing baobabs, and also singular princes, madcap adventurers, mirages that aren't mirages at all. In Abéché, for example, Prince Daoud tries to help himself to the palace. At first, this personage who thinks the French will put him on the throne of Ouaddaï comes, out of curiosity, with his court to inspect the hundreds of pieces unpacked outside his city walls. He is interested in the mirrors, the ceilings, the frescoed walls; he is tall, with rings on his fingers and silken, splendid lips. At one point, without explanation, he gives an order to halt. A canopy is unfurled overhead; seats are brought for the prince and his court, in which there is a French officer with a profoundly distant air. Shafik and Samuel sit down on their own chairs. Daoud waves for the two White Men to be brought seats, but Samuel protests and explains that to himself and his friend, these chairs are the most precious thing they have in all the world. "I've even heard that you white men sit down on chairs to do your necessaries," says the Ouaddaï prince with a laugh. "Naturally, and much more besides," replies Samuel, who embarks on the story of the bourgeois Beiruti who offered his wife a trip to Europe by boat as a wedding gift. Once aboard, he continues, the delighted wife takes up quarters in her luxury cabin. She has just enough time to display her admiration at the European-style bathroom with its gilded marble commode when she suddenly feels seasick from the swaying, for the ship has begun to pull away from the port of Beirut. Her husband has her brought up to the deck; they fan her, they speak to her, but no sooner does she open her eyes than she feels on the verge of fainting, and the husband, who has authority and a name, demands that he and his wife be put back on solid ground. There is much discussion, the captain himself is summoned, and orders that a lifeboat be lowered to the water. A few months later, Samuel concludes, the rich bourgeois Beiruti has the first European-style bathroom in all the Orient installed in his home, with a commode for bodily functions, which he offers to his wife in lieu of the wedding gift gone wrong.

When he is done, much rambling on ensues about the oddness of the Lebanese and women in general, but the French officer impassively declares, as if insidiously insinuating in Daoud's ear the poison of doubt, that a commode is also called a "throne" in French and quite possibly even in English. This casts a pall, and by the time the prince steps from the shade of his awning, a peculiar atmosphere has reigned for quite a spell. Moreover, from that day on, a metaphor begins spinning out its wicked filaments in Daoud's mind; for him, marriage becomes an allusion to his union with the French, which can lead only to a single conclusion: that wife, to whom a commode is being offered, can be none other than himself. This sends him into a fury, or else he pretends it does. He sends a message to the two Lebanese expressing his affrontedness and demanding reparation. Samuel and Shafik, to whom it seems clear all this is but a maneuver to confiscate the palace, nonetheless make the prince a gift of the chest inlaid with mother-of-pearl. But the next day two mounted guards burst into camp and hurl the chest unceremoniously into the dust. As things seem to taking a turn for the worse, Samuel persuades Shafik to strike camp, which they do under cover of night, and at dawn the vast caravan leaves the outskirts of town. Furious, Daoud sets out in pursuit. Samuel's riders, who have stayed behind, keep him from leaving the city; shots are exchanged, Gawad's riders employ their English rifles to great effect, and Daoud, who cannot engage them without compromising what he believes are his chances of being restored to the throne of Ouaddaï, orders his warriors to stand down.

Two days later, Samuel abandons his positions. At an oasis where he stops with his troops to spend the night, he dines with a Lebanese adventurer—yes, another one, who turns up out of nowhere on camelback in the middle of the savannah and introduces himself, in explorer's garb, with a monocle and a tic that keeps his nostrils aquiver. Accompanying him are three large black men, and he takes a seat beside the fire that Samuel's men have lit for dinner. He knows about Shafik Abyad's cargo, he's been hearing about it for months, and he makes Samuel a proposition: why don't his two fellow countrymen come with him and sell it to Suleiman Kurra, a powerful sheikh in Gimr, soon to be married, to whom he himself is bringing goods for the wedding.

"He will buy your palace to house his new wives," the Lebanese explorer assures Samuel.

"How many is he marrying at once?" asks Samuel, who doesn't like the looks of this man, for he has a slightly unbalanced stare and a disturbing smile, his stare and his smile never agreeing, the former blazing while the latter remains frozen, the latter unleashed without warning even as the former remains glum.

"He'll have his pick," says the man. "He'll soon be getting four slaves, and he'll choose his bride-to-be from among them."

So saying, he gives his very delicate nostrils a pinch.

"And meanwhile, he's putting them all up at his own house?" Samuel asks as the cries of foxes ring through the night.

"Why, of course," says the Lebanese man with the bizarre smile that has nothing to do with his face. "He'll put them up in the seraglio you sell him. He's buying children, girls he's having brought over from the heart of Equatoria. He'll let them grow up under his eye and then one day, he'll pick the prettiest one to marry."

And as he speaks, with a mocking air, he leans forward to pluck a mouthful of millet from a passing platter. Samuel watches him, taken aback, as the platters of rice and vegetables pass from hand to hand, and then the man adds, "At least this way, he can train them himself. It'll save him from ever being asked for a solid gold crapper, like in that story you tell everywhere you go."

And he bursts out laughing, then suddenly falls silent and looks at Samuel mischievously as a madman before going on: "Don't worry, I'll help you sell him that palace of yours. Trust me."

"I'm not worried in the slightest. And what are you going to sell Suleiman Kurra?"

"What he needs most for his wedding," says the Lebanese explorer, his stare unwavering but his smile cheery.

"And what is that, exactly?" Samuel insists.

"Women," says the Lebanese explorer, whose stare and smile match up for the first time, whose entire face is gleeful and gloating. A long silence follows, which he seizes upon, with an ambiguous gesture, to clean the monocle he never places over his eye.

"No doubt you know the French have serious punishments for slave traders in the region," Samuel says at last.

"I can take care of myself!" says the other man, letting the monocle fall.

And as if to punctuate his rejoinder, he waves at one of his black companions, with their martial stares. The man rises, disappears into the darkness of the oasis, then returns with a saddlebag from which he pulls, before those gathered in a circle, a strange potbellied object he places on the sand as he might a severed head. And only gradually does the nature of this trophy become clear to Samuel's incredulous eyes: it is the battered helmet of a Roman legionary from antiquity, standing on its neck guard and pointed ear guards like a shelled creature, empty, hollow, inert but inundated with the immeasurable mystery it represents, risen from the depths of time in the middle of the African desert, recalling the fabulous encounter between the black tribes and the crests, crimson capes, and eagles of Rome. It takes Samuel a moment for his memory to stir, and he remembers reading once, long ago, about legions gone to seek some mythic realm or another, who strayed and were lost forever in the deepest Africa.

"Where did you get that thing?" he asks his fellow countryman.

"From the sands of Dar al-Arba'in," says the other man, whose face has recovered the euphoric simultaneity of fixedness and motion. "Somewhere in the desert. There lie bones worn rougher than pumice, and weapons, and helmets."

"You went there?"

"Who can, without going mad? But I have my suppliers. And let me tell you, for a gift like this, the French officer in charge of the garrison at Gimr will always look the other way."

In the morning, the Lebanese explorer comes to see Samuel, with his half-frozen, half-animated air and quivering nostrils, monocle dangling uselessly from his French chemise. In answer to the question about his decision on last night's offer, Samuel tells him of course not, and as for any commission on the sale, sorry, that won't happen either. "However," he says, "I'd like very much to buy that Roman helmet from you." The Lebanese man hesitates, his whole face freezing in a moment of fleeting astonishment, then mobility returns at all once—to his blazing eyes, then his leftward-leaning smile. The man sighs, pouts—pure playacting on the his part, Samuel thinks—and indeed he finally comes out and says, all right, fine, I can't say no to a fellow countryman, but naturally it'll be quite expensive, even with the deal he's cutting Samuel. I don't want any deal, Samuel says, and an hour later, he's back on the road with his riders, with English gold and the helmet of a lost legionary wrapped up in fabric, dangling from the side of his mount like a trophy. But after just a few hours, he retraces his steps, and for three days circles the oasis, watching the trails to try to ambush the goods the Lebanese man with the monocle is waiting for. One day, with his binoculars, he spots a convoy coming from the east with great *utfas* nodding on the backs of several camels, attesting to the presence of women. The encounter is dramatic, Samuel's orders accompanied by the horses' snorts of impatience. Gawad also makes a few menacing gestures to his warriors, but their searches turn up nothing. The women beneath the canopies of the camel litters are merchants' wives returning from Khartoum, whose husbands let the White Man see them, as everyone takes him for a British soldier in civilian clothes. On the third day, they force a caravan transporting goods from Equatoria to a halt. But there are no women, only ivory, precious woods, and preposterous animals: green parrots and pink-buttocked baboons, in particular four females squealing and clucking in four cages. At the sight of them, Samuel bursts into laughter, then asks where the caravan is going.

"Dar Gimr," states the man in charge.

"Whom are these little monkeys meant for?"

"Suleiman Kurra," says their owner.

"Is Suleiman Kurra getting married?" Samuel asks.

The other man makes a face as if to say, how would I know?

"Did a Lebanese man arrange this deal?" Samuel insists.

"Yes," says the merchant. "Do you know him?"

"He's waiting for you at the oasis in Badr," Samuel replies. "But tell me one last thing. Is there a French garrison in Gimr?"

"Not at all. Gimr is a free sultanate."

"Then farewell."

*

Now, while Samuel is seeing to this little affair concerning the desert explorer, Shafik Abyad is making his way east when, on the third day, things take a bad turn and his camel drivers fall into their old habits, refusing to go any farther. The reason is clear. Samuel's unexplained departure has sown doubt among Shafik's men, who are now convinced the two White Men have gone their separate ways. Which means the guarantee that Samuel embodied, of wages at every step along the way, has vanished into thin air. Not to mention that the mysterious treasure from which Samuel would pull the deciding argument in any conversation had wound up exerting a powerful magnetism on them. It was at work on their dreams, and secretly fed their whisperings. Its tacit presence galvanized and reassured them, as if they went everywhere accompanied by a comforting force, an occult source of energy defended by dark warriors from Safa. And now the warriors have vanished along with Samuel, and explain as he might that they will return, it does Shafik Abyad no good. "Let us wait for them," one of the caravaners says at first, but Shafik refuses. They keep pressing on eastward one more day, and finally, mutiny breaks out; to test him, the men challenge Shafik to pay them for the past few days. When he refuses, they gather, hold a lengthy parley, and decide not only to change their route, but if Abyad resists, to abandon him by a well. Unable to impose his plans upon them, the Lebanese man finds himself forced to give in, such that just as Samuel is try-

ing to rejoin him by galloping eastward, he is being led
south despite himself, like a captain imprisoned on his
own vessel. But desperation drives him to a most singular
decision. On the very site of the mutiny, he leaves one of
the bronze-framed mirrors in hopes it will catch the eye
of Samuel's riders. Then a few hours later, he has a camel
driver loyal to him jettison one of the carved wooden
doors, and from then on, whenever he gets a chance, he
leaves a piece of his palace behind: easily spotted pieces
at first, parts of the Moorish-style pool, sculpted wood
from the roof, a chest, and then, by turns, sometimes a
striking object, a portion of mashrabiya, a section of frescoed wall, and sometimes numbered stones from walls
south, east, and west... For days and days he goes on like
this, sloughing the palace behind him, sowing it across
the savannah at the feet of boxwood hedges, beneath acacias, on the red and ochre sand, the long tail of a caravan
whose cargo its owner is liquidating with a belligerence
no longer motivated only by the desire to leave some
trace of his passing but also the will to avenge himself
on fate, to have done—coldly, meticulously—with this
entire affair. And as Shafik Abyad abandons his absurd
dream piece by piece, the caravaners head stubbornly
south, occupied with their own business, not suspecting a thing. Then, of course, they finally take notice and
another secret meeting is held. Some laugh and declare
it proof that Samuel is coming back to them. But others
protest and say that if the Safa warriors find their trail,

their vengeance will be terrible. A quarrel breaks out as Shafik is sitting beneath a baobab with a few faithful followers, and from a distance, he manages more or less to grasp that the mutineers are now convinced Samuel will return. Some think they'd be better off waiting for him, even if it means explaining themselves, while others think it'd be too risky, and suggest departing as soon as possible, leaving Abyad behind. Finally, they decide to try to reach the town of Wak, in Dar Tama.

And so they set out once more while, on his end, Samuel and his twenty-five warriors have been galloping toward the rising sun ever since the oasis in Badr. After three days, doubt sets in, they stop, go in circles, and begin exploring the various available trails—the one for Musbat, then the one for Bi'r Furāwīyah, and also the one going from Gimr to Teiga until, one afternoon, a group of riders get a shard of sunlight right in the eye from a singular piece of glass and find, where the path to Qumqum crosses the one to Dar Tama, the bronze-framed mirror leaning against an acacia. Its silvering, murkier than ever, can still reflect the desert path, the green and dusty stands of trees—and perhaps it has also reflected, in the past few days, gazelles galloping by, slow, snooping hyenas, and stilted ostriches. After this discovery, Samuel and his troops have only to push southward for a bit before they find, crowning a thicket of wild broom, one of the carved doors from Abyad's palace and then, a day's walk away, part of the green and turquoise Moorish-style fountain, forsaken under a baobab. "Something's wrong," Samuel says. When ashlar follows every half-day—block number 105 ("stateroom"), number 72 ("windowsill, women's divan"), and then number 42 ("bedrock, gallery wall")—he realizes what might have driven Shafik to act as he did, and quickens his pace, now passing without even stopping the other, ever more lavish pieces strewn across the savannah like old rags, and catches up with the caravan just as it is setting out again after the secret meetings and arguments.

Taking things back in hand inevitably involves some severity. The main leaders of the mutiny are driven out. Standing on a pile of canvas tent tarps, Samuel makes a scathing speech to the others, surrounded by the glowering faces of the Safa horsemen. But that night, seated at the table, he tells the story of the Lebanese explorer. Shafik laughs and makes jokes. He's started losing weight again, but his eyes recover a bit of cheer in Samuel's presence, and throughout the entire meal, the Roman helmet, set down like a ferocious table decoration, takes on strange aspects, ghostly or menacing depending on the whim of the fire they're eating next to, which sets their shadows dancing around them. When they are done, and Samuel announces that plans must be made to recover the cargo scattered across the savannah, Shafik's face grows somber once more, his gaze goes dark, and he declares firmly that it's out of the question, he's had enough, this time he's through and the palace will stay where it is, he's strewn it all about because he no longer wishes to hear of it. A bitter exchange breaks out; Samuel declares that they haven't done all this for nothing. But that's exactly what they've done, Shafik replies, and he's had enough, he's been an idiot, he's ruined himself, but that's how it is. Samuel insists that nothing is lost, one option still remains, maybe the best one, and after suffering Shafik's irony once more, an irony Shafik turns against himself before consenting to shut up and listen, Samuel declares that they still have an option: they'll sell the palace to the British government in Khartoum. For a moment, Shafik Abyad thinks he's being funny, and eyes Samuel with the same bitter irony.

"And what makes you think the English will want it?" he asks.

"I say they will," Samuel replies, "and I will buy it from you in their name right now."

"And what will you buy it with?"

"Colonel Moore's gold."

Shafik gives Samuel a good long stare to make sure he's serious about his intentions.

"That gold doesn't belong to you," he says at last. "You can't just spend it like that."

"I've been entrusted with it, and I will do with it as I see fit," Samuel replies. "If the government in Khartoum has anything to say about it later, well then, I shall keep the palace for myself. The English owe me five years' back wages, an enormous sum in hazard pay, and quite a few bonuses. I'll take my payment in the form of these goods."

As this is said in a way that brooks no reply, Abyad mutters something, then slowly starts to smile, till finally, with a laugh, the two men raise a toast and drink brackish water from wooden cups while all about them, cajoled by the flames, play shadows of acacias and broom.

In the days that follow, Samuel leads twenty-some camels back toward the intersection of the paths to Tama and Qumqum, salvaging the pieces scattered across the savannah. The first day, a fearsome rain falls upon the land, after which the desert suddenly appears restored and glistening, like a gleaming sword drawn from its sheath, like a torrent of color after months of unbroken dusty whiteness. The shaggy acacias seem to exult beneath a cleansed sky, and on the horizon, carved out in immaculate light, archipelagoes of baobabs look like legions of unmoving women hitching up their robes. In the heart of this miraculous setting, while evanescent verdure carpets the savannah, Samuel collects fragments of the wall frescoed with birds and fountains, the doors whose wood has suffered in the rain, and sections of the fountain with gilded arabesques, which he must go looking for in thickets of broom. On the second day, he has to stop a Baggāra family with their cows and haggle to buy back a painted, woodworked window the nomads found in their path and refuse to sell without compensation.

On the fifth day, not far from the intersection, Samuel's troop comes to a halt, for the scouts report that right under the same acacia where the tall mirror still stands, a pair of lions have made their home. A few shots from a rifle might scare them off, but Samuel rejects this idea. As they are upwind, he approaches on foot, Gawad in tow, and then, lying in the sand in the shade of a small arbutus tree, he gazes upon the animals at length through his binoculars. He sees them lolling about, stretching, making silent conversation, their magisterial languor blending in with the formidable silence their presence creates. Far from being frightened by their reflections in the mirror, they seem from time to time to stare at their own images, patient and placid, the male even yawning wide, and the female often and openly turning her back on herself. After a few long hours of spying on them Samuel gives the order to fire a few shots, which is soon done. After rising ceremoniously and taking a long sniff of their surroundings, necks outstretched and muzzles in the air, the lions finally take their leave, and the mirror's reclamation is the final episode in the first long odyssey of Shafik Abyad's Arabian palace. Three days later, the caravan carrying it almost in its entirety sets out resolutely east again, exiting the western provinces and, after overtaking the Marrah Mountains and crossing northern Kurdufan with its infinitely chalk-white light, through twilights that lay shadows down like assegai, and mornings full of limpid gaiety, the caravan comes at the end of a fortnight's travel within view of Khartoum and at last, enters Omdurman—slowly, with the somber, melancholy pride of a great ship returning to its home port.

6

FROM VAGUE ACCOUNTS, CROSS-CHECKING, AND THE
conclusions that may be drawn from what happened
next, Samuel Ayyad leaves western Sudan and resur-
faces in Khartoum around the middle of 1914. He does
not arrive impromptu, but has himself announced, and
Colonel Moore comes to wait for him personally in a
tilbury in the middle of the souq in Omdurman, the
caravan's final stop, whereupon he takes Samuel to Khartoum. For two days, Samuel does not set foot outside the
house where he has been installed, which he shares with
a captain from the intelligence service. Languorously, he
rediscovers the pleasure of sleeping in a bed, of baths,
of eau de toilette on his face, and also the voluptuous
indulgence of lying on a soft mattress all day long, legs
elevated and feet placed against the wrought-iron foot-
board, reading the forty or fifty letters he's received over
all these years from his parents and sisters in order, one
after another. For two days, he does nothing else; then
he writes a few letters in turn. On the third day, Moore
rolls up and, heckling him, declares with an astonished,
merry look in his eye that it's high time he was debriefed.

Samuel says he has nothing to wear but his old thread-bare suits. Moore sends an army tailor over, and at this moment, as if the news he's finally opened his doors has been announced, members of the newfound Lebanese community in Khartoum begin turning up to see him, all arrivals from the recent years, small shopkeepers, a broker by the name of Georges Khayyat who will later become one of the city's major landlords, and also Elias Dagher, an agricultural engineer that Lebanese industrialists in Cairo have hired, who agreed to come to Khartoum under one and only one condition—that a piano be brought over for his wife. Which was done, on a small steamboat, before the clumsy Sudanese laborers, just as they were unloading it, got tangled up in their movements, and howling powerlessly, bickering furiously with one another, let the handsome instrument slip into the Nile, at the bottom of which it has rested ever since.

For lack of diversion, but also because of the reputation that precedes him, everyone comes to see my grandfather. They're proud of him, impressed by his weathered skin, and a gaze that seems to have taken on something like a depth equal to the vast spaces they have long surveyed. This confers upon him the aura of an adventurer, and they do not notice the mocking glint in his eye, which he tempers in their presence. On the other hand, he tempers it less with Moore. The colonel's joy and volubility seems to kindle his own vivacity. For after the tenth day, he has two new suits—a bit military, perhaps, but they deprive him of an excuse to stay home any longer, so off he goes to his debriefing at government headquarters, where he spends long hours in Moore's office, telling stories of tribal warfare, abolished chiefdoms, and restored sultanates, while in the anteroom captains, supplicants, and civil servants wait, now and again catching a burst of laughter from the colonel. For laugh he does, that Colonel Moore; he tells Samuel that according to one report from the French services intercepted two years ago, when Samuel was with the sultan of Safa, inhabitants of the western regions called him the White Sultan: "You were the White Sultan, and your friend's name was Abyad," Abyad meaning white in Arabic. "The French must not have known where they stood anymore." And that makes Moore laugh, as do the stories about Shafik: "Now that's the first time I've ever heard of a turtle wanting to sell its own shell! That Abyad of yours is a character straight out of La Fontaine!" Samuel, familiar with British humor, laughs more at Moore's laughter than at his schoolboy jokes. Then, in one of his abrupt reversals, the colonel turns serious again; through the door to the office, from which not a sound can now be heard, the supplicants and the captains outside can tell concentration has returned. At this moment, the colonel is telling Samuel that while, admittedly, his actions in Safa have driven the French to take Ouaddaï, they have also allowed both powers to settle the borders of their zones, which is very good for what will come next, after the war currently under way, and here the two men are, discussing the war in Europe.

All this goes on for hours without the colonel alluding in any way to the gold in Samuel's charge. And yet when he came in, Samuel set down the remaining bags of gold on the table before him. As Moore has paid them no mind, Samuel finally adopts a more solemn bearing and launches into the part of his report concerning such matters. Moore falls silent, listening almost reluctantly. His eyes soon begin to quiver, on the brink of distraction, until the moment Samuel explains he bought Abyad's palace in the name of the government in Khartoum. Moore keeps looking at him in that flighty way, and Samuel thinks that the colonel hasn't been listening. But the colonel rises, and then, as if dismissing the question with a wave of his hand, he announces that Samuel can keep the palace, it's all his, and the rest of the gold, too, that's all been written off, an unrecoverable outlay that might've funded the campaign against Bellal or helped other princes against the French hegemony, or even, he adds with a sigh, to arrange for other grandiose spectacles of princely warfare. And with these words, he crosses to the office door and opens it to the captains, supplicants, and civil servants who instantly snap to attention when he appears.

A few days later, Samuel receives, in addition, the balance due for his years of service. He begins going to headquarters again daily, where he drafts a few notes on affairs in the west, giving his written opinion on what position to take regarding the new, still-independent sultanates in light of the new war, and this allows him to become acquainted with the war, reading newspapers and conversing with intelligence officers. Now and again, he remembers he is rich; he dreams of the resin-scented pine woods of Souk el Gharb, the town where he was born, the summer winds over Beirut, and he is racked with violent nostalgia for his sisters' laughter and the soft sheets in the bedrooms of his family's house. One morning, he goes in to see Colonel Moore, and announces he is going home. Moore reminds him that leaving for Lebanon might be a tad difficult at the moment, for all intelligence and speculation leads one to believe that the Ottoman Empire will soon enter the war on Germany's side. Since this hasn't happened yet, Samuel replies that he'll give it a try anyway, and leaves. But he doesn't just leave like that, by boat, with two trunks and a new suit and hat, surrounded by respect from sailors and other travelers, like an immigrant who's made it in the world, impatient to return home in triumph. No, for his baggage is far more cumbersome: Abyad's palace, which he has decided to bring home with him. It takes him three days, in a worn-out uniform, to organize the thousand pieces of the seraglio, piled in an open-roofed warehouse, between four adobe walls, and perfunctorily draped in tarps. Then he supervises their loading onto two steamers he's chartered and finally it is his turn to board, while

Moore and his officers, and the full complement of the Lebanese community, wave from the dock.

Getting the palace down the Nile is naturally much easier than promenading it around on camelback across the savannah. For ten days, the two ships sail placidly on calm waters, and Samuel spends his hours on a rattan chaise lounge and dines at the captain's table, discussing Pharaonic and Celtic civilizations with the Irishman, as well as the conflict in Europe. Then, hair ruffled, wearing a shirt the wind amusingly balloons, he remains on deck, leaning on the railing, watching the banks of the river, eyes misting over at the bright light bouncing from the sand, the rocks, the palm groves, trying to make out in the horizon's mirages the pyramids of the black-skinned pharaohs of Meroë and the Temple of Soleb. One morning, off Dongola, they pass a wheezing, rattle-trap steamer, overloaded with Sudanese in white robes, who wave from afar. In Wadi Halfa, where he sets foot on land, he is welcomed by Selim Atiyah, chief medical officer of the British Army hospital, a Lebanese man he has heard tell of in Khartoum. It is he who apprises Samuel that the Ottoman Empire has entered the war. Samuel converses with Atiyah and his wife on the terrace of their house where, at night, during dinner, the wind never stops playing the clown, always blowing out the lantern in the middle of the table. Atiyah is a stocky, mischievous man with an upward-curling mustache, who keeps in reach at all times a notebook where he jots down little *zajals* in Lebanese vernacular, inspired by the situation at hand, whether Turkey's entrance into the war or the wedding of a Wadi Halfa dignitary, or a pimple growing under his pretty's wife's nose, which he finds only increases her charm. He tells Samuel that going to Beirut now amounts to a risk and suggests he stay with them. Samuel declares that he will go on to Cairo, and departs; from the landing stage, Selim Atiyah waves to him and then, on his way home, consigns to three amusing couplets his memories of an evening when the wind invited itself over for dinner, and of that singular fellow countryman navigating the Nile with, in lieu of luggage, a palace in pieces.

So Samuel leaves once more, and it takes him another five days to reach Cairo. In Abu Simbel, standing on the shoulder of Rameses, he give the imposing pharaoh's ear a friendly rub—it's twice his size—while down below, three English ladies picnic beneath their broad hats. In Luxor, he spends a whole day strolling around the temples, among the living pillars, amidst the forest of symbols he studies dumbfounded, such that all that night and the next day, images of ibises and men with the heads of cats and falcons seem to be imprinted on his retinas, coming to life and commingling against the backdrop of his eyelids whenever he shuts them. Next to parade by are slow and verdant banks of Upper Egypt, with their norias, their donkeys, their fellahs, and their pyramids, and finally, with his two boatfuls of a palace he now wonders what he's going to do with, he reaches Cairo.

At first, he looks around for a warehouse to store his cumbersome baggage, and finds one near the port's customshouse. For two days, he stays on board the steamer, overseeing the unloading. Once it is done, he has himself driven directly to Shepheard's Hotel. Upon stepping inside and walking through the vast salons, beneath the domes and colonnades, amidst clientele that gives off an impression of being on *villeggiatura* somewhere in Normandy, he feels a moment's hesitation, then remembers he is rich—very rich. At the front desk, his Western suit and billionaire adventurer's air impress the staff, whose stiffness relents a bit when Samuel speaks a few words of Arabic—Lebanese Arabic, admittedly, but it's enough to establish a respectful, less distant sympathy between them, taken up in turn by the servile attentiveness of a legion of bellhops in operetta outfits who lead him, from stairway to elevator, all the way to his room. He still has two whole days to lounge about in his massive bed, his marble bathroom, and the hotel's salons, in which he sometimes feels like an intruder at a very exclusive English club where reading London newspapers and savoring cigars constitute the liturgy. He, too, reads papers, eavesdropping discreetly, from deep within armchairs, on the conversations of the gentlemen around him about the war and the Ottoman Empire's entrance into the conflict. The guests, for their part, examine him indiscreetly, which he finds amusing. An Englishwoman in a flowered hat spreads the notion that he may be a secret agent. A Belgian cannon dealer with a lively imagination, or else up on the latest gossip, whispers that he may be Slatin Pasha, the Austrian general who recently left the Sudan, but has remained in Egypt incognito by the grace of the British generals' friendship for him. Finally, a Russian colonel, the Tsar's envoy to the Egyptian government, has a chat with Samuel one morning at breakfast. Between marmalade toast and a sip of tea, Samuel sums himself up in a nutshell, but the story of a Protestant Lebanese man who served the British Army in nameless sultanates leaves the Russian perplexed, while it only rekindles the imaginations of the prestigious hotel's guests.

*

Meanwhile, Samuel embarks on several inquiries, trying to find a way to Beirut despite news of the French and British navies' recent blockade off the Lebanese coast. At first, he tries in vain to send a few telegrams, then goes to the Egyptian Ministry of War and above all the Savoy Hotel, where the general headquarters of the British Army is to be found, and where marble walls, rugs, and chandeliers serve as the backdrop to the officers' hushed comings-and-goings. His name and Moore's are enough of an *Open, Sesame* to give him access to captains in the know and even a colonel in intelligence. But the end result of all he hears is that it is no longer possible to go to Beirut. While waiting to find a solution, he visits a few old friends of his father's, such as Khalil Tabet, one of the pioneers of the Arab cultural renaissance of the early twentieth century, who runs the famous newspaper *al-Mokattam*, for which Nassib Ayyad once wrote articles on the Arab poetry revival. Then he goes to see Khalil Courbane, a poet of unbridled lyrical impulses and master of the postromantics in the Oriental literary renaissance. Courbane receives him in a luxurious villa in Maadi that Farid Pasha, the king's brother, has placed at his disposal. Samuel waits patiently in a salon with European furniture until a door opens and out comes Courbane, arms flung wide, murmuring words of welcome. He is thin and very lavishly attired, with an ascot and gold cuff links, and starts out with small, fond comments, which Samuel finds excessive, about his old friendship with Nassib Ayyad. Then he moves on to Samuel himself, whom he has heard about, whom he questions and listens to, an elbow on the arm of his chair, leaning toward the young man like a bishop in audience. But quite soon he stops listening, distracted by a butler who seems from his mysterious cycle of comings and goings to be reporting something of capital importance to him, no doubt that his calash is waiting, for the poet indeed seems dressed for an outing. Samuel immediately excuses himself, rising, and Courbane, without insisting, likely for fear of missing his morning programming, begs

CHARIF MAJDALANI

him to come back, we can discuss it another time, and I'll show you my latest work. But Samuel leaves with no intention of ever returning.

What Samuel cannot suspect is that Khalil Courbane immediately embarks on spreading word of his presence in Cairo to every club and society salon of the Lebanese community where he spends his days and evenings. This community has in fact heard tell of Samuel already, and his nickname the "White Sultan" sets them dreaming. We might for instance imagine that, during a dinner hosted by Alfred Soussa, building contractor and assistant to the Khedive, after someone (most likely a young woman, one of those girls of sixteen or seventeen, who in Cairo are said never to be at a loss for words) has asked what this Samuel Ayyad is like, and Courbane has declared that he is very young and highly cultured, Yvonne Soussa tells "the great poet" that they must invite him someday, it would be the least they could do, before adding, "Tell him to come next Thursday, Khalil, for the dinner with Rida Pasha." And the great poet replies—in French, of course, a language he must have had to learn in order to communicate in the fiercely Francophile Lebanese salons of Cairo, but which he continues to speak with an affected accent, immoderately rolling his Rs, as if on purpose—"But my dea*rrr* Yvonne, that's none of my business, inviting him is enti*rrr*ely up to you." And so it is that three days later, an envelope addressed to Samuel Ayyad arrives at Shepheard's, inside of which a splendid scalloped invitation card from Monsieur and Madame Soussa requests the pleasure of his company (all in French, of course) at a dinner in honor of the Minister of War at the Villa Soussa on the eighteenth of March.

It must be remembered that Cairo at the time, though far from Europe, is the first city to rival Paris and Vienna for its soirées, the richness of its salons, and above all the power of its economic and financial elite. And just like Paris or Vienna, high society there is highly hierarchized. If most families, and thus the city's most prominent society salons, are Syro-Lebanese in origin, the inner circle belongs to dynasties that emigrated before the middle of the nineteenth century and built their fortunes in the first era of Egypt's modernization—like the Sakakini, Egypt's first manufacturers, treasurers, and ministers to the viceroys and then the khedives, or the Soussas, builders of the Suez Canal and customs leaseholders at the port of Suez. This inner circle consists of close friends to the khedives and European consuls, especially the famous John Baring, who can be seen at every dinner in their palaces on the Ezbekieh. The second circle consists of families who arrived in the second half of the century, like the Debbas, the Sabbaghs, and the Canaans. Movement between these first and second circles is continual, as are marriages, like the famous marriage between Georges bey Soussa and Yvonne Sabbagh, celebrations for which rivaled the parties the khedive threw for the inauguration of the Suez Canal in the presence of Empress Eugenia. But in its coats of arms, its family history, and its association with princely European families, the inner circle possesses a patina more recent families do not, which of course allows for the free play of hushed snobbery, veiled allusions, and pettiness of pecking order.

At any rate, one might indeed wonder how, under such conditions, a young adventurer can succeed in stirring or astonishing his audience. Except that it is precisely because he is young and an adventurer, and the socialites seem to see a kind of grace attending to his every movement, a force and energy in his gaze that scours clean and intimidates. And then, of course, there is the aura, for starters, that his reputation as a founder of sultanates confers upon him, and his nickname the "White Sultan," which result in his being welcomed, right from that first night at the Soussas, like Garibaldi in the salons of Palermo, or Kosciuszko in Paris. The ladies are almost sorry he's not in his savannah outfit, dusty and virile, eyes shining and beard weary. But he dons a tuxedo and lace-up shoes, and I'd like to think he tops off all this elegance with a spot-on touch, a killer detail, one that draws voracious looks from the young women, which is to say: breeding, which he gets from his family and deploys in all its Victorian panoply. They await him with curiosity, and here he is, arriving, accompanied by Courbane, who's picked him up in his coupé, and of course, his way of greeting—that perfectly calculated twist of his chest just as he kisses Yvonne Soussa's hand—his natural-ness ("Almost royal, don't you think, my dear?" Madame Sakakini, mother to the Countess Debbaneh, will later say once he's left), that naturalness in his about-face toward Alfred-bey, the smiles and murmured words of thanks for the welcome that ring with impeccable right-ness in the ears of his hosts—all this makes him almost as splendid in the imaginations of the ladies and young women as a highwayman or the Count of Monte Cristo. After which, he is constantly invited to dinners, garden parties, even five o'clock teas, a rite of which this fiercely Francophile society is so oddly fond. Those close to the king and the friends of European princes approach him as if he were a rare and precious object, a representative from a race of men who have had great power among the blacks and deep within the most savage kingdoms and who, as a result, have seen the strangest sights humanity has to offer. He smokes long cigars while discussing the war in Europe with Fernand Debbas, whose fingers are thick with rings, and Halim Sayegh, who while listening never stops looking into his whisky glass and clinking the ice cubes in his impatience to be done listening so he himself can stop being silent and start to talk. Samuel drinks white wine, which he hates, telling tales of his wanderings in the Ouaddaï and ill-tempered camels to a French consul and a Russian plenipotentiary who eye him as if he were recounting crossing the Alps with Han-nibal's elephants. And one night, at the Soussas', sitting in an armchair across from Georges Khayyat, who whispers as if he were spilling state secrets, Samuel listens as the industrialist explains that his favorite dish, which an old Nubian once made for him long ago, and to which he has since brought his own personal touch, are giraffe testicles stuffed with coriander and black olives from Lebanon.

But none of this distracts Samuel from his basic goal, and twice a week, he heads for the Savoy, where he first hears word of an Arab revolt against the Ottoman Empire. He tries to make sense of the information coming in from Damascus and Arabia, and ends up offering his help in drafting reports on a possible uprising in Syria. This brings him closer to the ground, and so he tries to sort out possibilities for getting all the way to Beirut. Of course, as an agent, or even a spy, there's always a way. But with a palace carved up into almost a thousand pieces, the way is much less obvious. Nonetheless, every morning he works in his room at Shepheard's, and soon concludes that getting to Beirut by boat has become utterly unthinkable, and getting there overland has become impossible as well, as all access to Palestine via the Sinai is now part of the front. And it is no doubt at this moment that an astonishing conviction takes hold of him: the best way of reaching Lebanon, even if it is also the most convoluted, would be from behind, via Syria, first by way of Arabia, where the revolt has just opened the doors to the Allies, but also where the tribal allegiances and the chiefdoms' alliances are so volatile that the frontlines of the war are still hazy and entirely porous.

As he works on refining this outlandish route, the window is open before him and looks out on the pines and magnolias of the hotel grounds. Behind him, on an armchair, is one of the countless suits he's had made by a celebrated Armenian tailor of Cairo, which he will wear to Syro-Lebanese society gatherings, some of which are renowned to this day, like the garden party on the grounds of the Villa Sabbagh, where three chimpanzees unexpectedly turn up in the middle of everything, gamboling among the tables, upending platters, and squelching about in the sauces, pursued by *sofragis* in tarbooshes to the cheers of men and the screams of women aquiver with horror and fascination. Or like that lunch in the Sayeghs' salon where General Archibald Murray, commander in chief of the British forces in Egypt, is announced and, upon walking in, just as everyone is trying look composed, trips on a fringe of the vestibule rug. Unable to regain his balance, he pitches headlong into the room and ends his pathetic tumble on his knees between the legs of the elderly Countess Raymonde Sayegh, who calmly pats him on the shoulder and expresses her regrets at finding him *there* instead of with one of the charming young women in attendance around her, and everyone that day agrees on one thing: the countess has a positively deadpan sense of humor, but it took seventy-five years to notice. Or even that evening at the Sakakinis, when a globe of glass inexplicably falls from a massive chandelier over the well-laid dining room table, drops right into a green and red Limoges soup tureen, and instantly reduces it to smithereens, spilling, among the other platters of silver and porcelain on the damask tablecloth, the thick, greenish, *mulukhiyah* stew in which strange gelatinous shapes are afloat, and here Yvette Sakakini, laughing in tears, reveals that these are gazelles' eyes, and she was trying to imitate Chinese soups. In front of fifty guests who at first hang on her every word, and are then irresistibly overtaken by the same wild contagious laughter, she manages between hiccups to confess that it was a surprise she was saving for her guests, but that God himself foiled her dreadful jest by dropping that pendant in the soup, and she says all this without realizing that she, a woman almost old enough to be Samuel's mother, has let herself slump on his shoulder, clutching him with undue familiarity, the better to double up with laughter, such that Samuel finally says in French: "Really now, Madame! All the gazelles in your herd are staring at us!" and Yvette Sakakini's laughing fit is off to a fresh start.

7

DURING THE ARAB REVOLT IN AL-HEJAZ, THE BRITISH and the French supplied Prince Faisal's army with logistical support and equipment, sometimes even naval and aerial backing, but they committed very few soldiers to the ground. The reason for this was simple: the pressing need to preserve the insurrection's native aspect, not to compromise their victory by sending in troops that would've been seen as instruments of future foreign domination. This strategic option was championed, as we know, by Thomas Edward Lawrence, at first against his own superiors, and then against the French, more inclined to send in forces to support, even replace, Prince Faisal's in the war against the Turks. And so the conflict in Al-Hejaz retained its aspect of a great tribal uprising, as Lawrence wished, and did not turn into a war of positions, with fixed and well-defined fronts. But it is clear that not all the tribes of Al-Hejaz involved themselves in the revolt, at least not right away. One of the fundamental problems Faisal and his family were confronted with was the difficulty of rallying the various confederations of Arabian tribes and their chieftains, who all swung between the Hashemite family and the Turks. If the Jouhaina, for instance, came round right away, and the Howeitat waited to see how events shook out before joining up with Faisal and drawing other groups to him, the Billi, whose central position in Al-Hejaz was strategic, remained recalcitrant about allying themselves with the prince. Even when certain major chieftains decided to join the revolt or, on the contrary, to stay out of it, or even to remain faithful to the Turks, lesser chieftains could make the exact opposite decision, the only true issue at stake for tribes being to obtain money and guns and the wartime possibility of substantial spoils, which drove them to throw in their lot with the highest bidder. In such a situation, the maps of military operations were highly unstable. In all the war, only two fixed points were beyond dispute. The first was the city of Medina, where the Ottomans had concentrated their troops meant to wrest back control of Arabia, and where said troops were being lackadaisically besieged by Arab tribes. The second, more sprawling, ran along the train line across Al-Hejaz—that is, six hundred and twenty miles, from the Syrian steppes to the city of Medina—where Arab tribes, accompanied or commanded by British officers specialized in explosives, proceeded with sabotage, blowing up bridges and derailing trains. As for the rest, Al-Hejaz, nominally under Ottoman rule, was in reality controlled by tribes rallied to the revolt, which allowed for the free passage of individuals and caravans north and south, between Al-Hejaz and Syria—and thus allow for a crossing toward Lebanon.

It is on this final point that Samuel's conversations with the members of Arab Bureau turn, especially from the moment a letter signed by a certain General Moore reaches him at Shepheard's, inviting Samuel to join him at the Savoy the next day. Samuel naturally has his doubts as to the sender's identity, but when he shows up at the Savoy, he is reassured—it's the same old Moore, since promoted and now in charge of directly liaising between the Arab Bureau and the Ministry of War in London. On the balcony of the general's bedroom, overlooking the Nile where the feluccas seem as slow, indolent, and patient as the fellahs and their donkeys in the fields of Upper Egypt, the two men once more find themselves discussing tribal warfare and old-fashioned battles. In speaking of Arabia, Moore cites the Umayyads and the cavalcades of Arab riders beneath their green banners, out to conquer the world. But Samuel protests. His potential interest in all this is that such cavalcades might lead him to Beirut, and on that score, Moore is more reserved. He is constantly interrupted by orderlies who knock, enter, hand him letters, telegrams, and notes, then leave again. Moore is patient, takes whatever new document he is given, issues orders, and resumes: Now, where were we? Ah yes, how to reach Beirut, and he makes a funny face because the French, already hostile to the Arab Revolt qua revolt, and more in favor of an Allied intervention in

Al-Hejaz, will never agree to let Faisal's Bedouins reach Beirut: Lebanon is theirs, they want to make it an independent state.

Naturally, Samuel is happy to hear these words; no doubt he is silent for a moment too long, a bit dazzled inside by such news, and that is when Moore's eye turns metallic and fixed.

"I can tell you like the idea. Even if the French are the ones carrying it out, and they're willing to break their promises to us in order to do so!"

Then his gaze suddenly softens, grows more affectionate, and the general goes on: "Anyway, it won't keep you from reaching Beirut with all your baggage. But you're taking a significant risk."

"It would be, were I still a British liaison officer," Samuel replies. "But now I'm just a private citizen, and the caravan will in fact be my best cover."

Moore's gaze hardens once more, then relaxes until it's positively merry.

"So you think the Arab Bureau will furnish you with a means of setting foot in Arabia?" he says. "Not at all, my dear chap. Goodness me, whatever for? No, I'm the one who'll be doing that—personally. But in your opinion, what other way would I have to do so apart from sending you out as a liaison officer again, eh? Tell me, what choice do I have?"

And faced with silence from Samuel, who is eagerly awaiting the rest of what he has to say, he adds, "None at all, of course. And so it's as a liaison officer you will go, and you'll likely have a mission. That will be your cover. Until you can slip away. I'll do this for you. It's a way of returning the favor you did me in Darfur."

*

Samuel leaves for Suez a fortnight later—the time it takes Fernand Debbas, whose ships are providing the passage between Suez and Jeddah, to make the army's administrative services process the thousand pieces of the palace as cargo headed for Al Wajh, a coastal city where Faisal's tribes have gathered, and Samuel has been assigned. He sets out wearing a British uniform without insignia or a tie, confusing the soldiers at endless military checkpoints along the train line. At headquarters in Suez, he gets odd looks when he shows up. But when he states his identity, the bored or disdainful looks immediately give way to a rigid standing at attention, visible even in the facial features of an individual seated behind a desk. And at the same time, with greater respect, he is asked to wait; a noncommissioned officer puts through a phone call right in front of him, and with extreme politeness, he is conducted toward the offices of the naval staff. He then waits another fortnight before boarding a naval escort vessel headed for Al Wajh. On deck, several military automobiles are tied down, among them a telegraph communications car. A captain in the signals corps explains how it works, sitting with him in the cabin before an enormous chart with a thousand holes and hundreds of wires and pins. When Samuel steps outside again, the night sky seems immense to him. He spends part of the night watching Arabia's dark shores parade past, and the reflections of the ship's lights skim the opaque surface of the water beside him. Then he goes to bed. The next day at dawn, the vessel enters the port of Al Wajh, a small market town consisting of poor houses in a low line of unlimewashed stone, overlooked by an ancient fortress, hardly any higher, crouching on a kind of acropolis behind the town.

If at first Al Wajh offers up a far from heartening spectacle, it is nevertheless at that moment the focal point of the entire war in Arabia; for over a month now, Faisal's troops and all the tribes that have rallied to his cause have gathered there and are camping nearby. Which explains the hustle and bustle at the only pier in the port, and along the town's main street, the joy of poor shepherds in rags with their scrawny goats, the presence of barefoot Bedouins, and also a few soldiers in Western garb. "Members of an Anglo-Egyptian unit," explains Captain Covington, who's come to greet Samuel at the landing stage and takes him on foot through Al Wajh, past houses of flaking roughcast and a few nomad tents. Samuel isn't very surprised to see Covington again, he knows a number of British officers from the Sudan now serve as advisors in Arabia. As for Covington, he has heard of Samuel's adventures. The two colleagues leave town by the southern gate, chatting as they go, followed by an Egyptian soldier carrying Samuel's luggage. It's so humid Samuel says he feels like he's been dunked in a tub of viscid, lukewarm water. "It'll be better in the hills," Covington replies. "Not a whole lot," he admits, "but more bearable at any rate." On the other side of the low, worn-down wall, horses are waiting, and a few minutes later, the two officers reach Prince Faisal's encampment in the heights. There, the spectacle is surprising and grandiose in an entirely different way. Hundreds of tents of all sizes—stateroom tents, chieftain's tents, tribal tents, military tents—are spread out over various slopes and topped by oriflammes slowly waving in a slightly less waterlogged sea wind. Between these different levels, a steady traffic of men from all tribes, camels, horses, and mules gives an impression of perpetual motion, a place of hectic labor. And on the highest ridge Prince Faisal's tents sit enthroned beneath their gleaming banners.

*

Of course, I could have conjured up this encampment from imagination, but I see it through the eyes of Thomas Edward Lawrence as he describes it in his epic of the Arab movement. If, right from the start, I set myself the task of telling Samuel Ayyad's story from the little I know, one of the things I've always known is precisely that he met Prince Faisal and Lawrence himself, probably just once, and I like to think that it happened in the camp at Al-Wajh, for the broad outlines from which I am reconstructing my grandfather's story all converge on this place. So I will say that Covington has saved him a spot in his own tent, where Samuel receives instructions directly from the Arab Bureau and Moore. Then, in the afternoon or evening of his arrival, he is ushered into the tent where Prince Faisal receives guests. I imagine there are a few legendary characters there, like Rassim and Faiz el Ghusein, the two hotheaded Damascene advisors, or Colonel Aziz Ali el-Misri, the Ottoman army defector, or even the mysterious Franco-Algerian Captain Mohamed Ould Raho. And then, of course, there is Lawrence, and this is where the meeting that the Ayyad family will zealously treasure in its memory, and which, from Samuel's adventure, will remain after almost all the rest has faded away, takes place—although it was, I believe, of no consequence. But I have heard it told so often that I will do it the honor of telling it again. Here they are, face-to-face: the man who would become my grandfather, with his dancing eyes and stubborn tuft of hair, in military attire undone by the heat and the humidity, and Lawrence, in his white Bedouin robes and Arabian headgear, barefoot and refractory. They shake hands, exchange a few words—what about, I don't know—Beirut, perhaps, or the Syrian Protestant College which Lawrence is familiar with, perhaps the adventures in Darfur, how would I know? And that's that. Lawrence doubtless cannot rid himself of his mistrust of the Lebanese, much less of the Christians among them, and Samuel, according to what my mother often told me, could not keep from thinking that Lawrence really didn't look Arab at all, not that his costume didn't become him, or made him look like an extra in an Orientalist set at the Cairo Opera—quite the opposite, he was even too handsome bathed in a whiteness that further refined his features, but his robe quite simply seemed too big for him. No doubt that was a minor detail, but since the two men were never to see each other again, that is how the memory has remained, and eighty years later, was passed down to me.

Afterward, Samuel is invited to approach Faisal, who bids him sit to his left. Now, Faisal is quite fond of the Lebanese. Their mountain and its snows may have been, for him as for all Arabs, a kind of lantern lifted in the distance, even if he no doubt knew already, more or less, when he was in Al-Wajh, that he would never reign there. And so I imagine that, in his princely slenderness, and with quite gentle gestures nonetheless ringed by an aura of unyielding will, he speaks to Samuel, asks him about his name, then recalls the Bani Ayyad tribe, a clan of the Howeitat confederation. Samuel then alludes to old family genealogies according to which the Ayyads were descended from Arab Christian tribes before Islam, and wonders if he hasn't, among the Howeitat, cousins very distantly removed. Faisal smiles, his retinue watches Samuel with curiosity, after which other guests come into the tent and Samuel drifts off. Early that night, he is sitting on the edge of the mound where the British officers' tents are, gazing into the night at the town of Al-Wajh, and the lights of British ships at anchor. All around him are the hums and murmurings of camp, fires lit on every level, peopling the hillside with shifting shadows and songs both near and far. No sooner does the next morning dawn, in the dust and damp that turn every waking body into a kind of mass of thick, oozing liquid, than he finds Faisal's army beside Covington and makes the acquaintances of the Egyptian soldiers. In the tent he shares with the captain, he studies rough maps of the region. He leaves on horseback for the nearby mountains to see what they look like, then returns and spends his days worrying when his cargo will reach port. Meanwhile, he pays a visit to a merchant in town named Hussein el Mawlud, Fernand Debbas's correspondent to whom the goods are nominally addressed, and whom Samuel is paying generously as a frontman. After three weeks, the bundled-up palace has arrived, but Samuel cannot leave yet; he has been ordered to wait for a mission. For a month, maybe more, he receives no instructions, nor does the army move at all. Now and then, tribal chieftains come to swear their allegiance or simply suss out the situation; then suddenly, at any time of day, there'll be a sudden burst of panic: Bedouins, soldiers, animals left to themselves—all will turn in the direction others are running, a fight has broken out between two clans, or a clash between rival lords, and each time, it is Faisal's intervention that restores order.

But soon, news from the fronts confirms that the Ottomans in Medina are about to try to retreat north-ward, and as a result, things are set in motion. Ordnance units leave on operations against the rail lines to disrupt the retreat, and then Mohammed Ould Raho is reported out there with small detachments, and finally Samuel receives his orders. He is to go and support Captain Rosemond, who is having a hard time taking action on the railway in the region around Bir Suheila because the tribes there refuse to help him, though in theory they have sworn allegiance to Faisal. In studying the maps, Samuel notices that Bir Suheila is ideally situated north-east of Al-Wajh, on the other side of the railway line, in a sector where the tribes still aren't very reliable, but it looks easier to head north from there than anywhere else. He's not sure whether to see in this another helpful nudge from the incredible General Moore, but never-theless he smiles in gratitude. Two days of preparations prove sufficient, and there he is, on his way, at the head of twenty Bedouins from a Howeitat clan close to those in the region around Bir Suheila, under the command of Hamid Ibn Mansour el Hawli. Accompanying him is also a British sergeant specializing in explosives and four Egyptian soldiers trained in the use of a machine gun, as well as five mules carrying five hundred rifles. In his luggage are three thousand gold sovereigns, to aid in his discussions with reluctant tribes. It's become a habit; he is considered qualified for such support negotiations. To top it all off, in a so-called happy coincidence, a caravan is setting out for Oum el Sarmad at this very moment. It is headed by Hussein's cousin Fahim el Mawlud, and Samuel easily arranges for it to leave at the same time as he does, since Oum el Sarmad is twenty miles to the north of Bir Suheila.

*

And so it begins with a long march through the mountains, on paths that reveal, with every summit, at every turn, spectacular monuments of basalt, mammoth peaks, tablelands fit for the feasts of giants. Samuel mounts an animal Faisal has offered him and rides alongside Ibn Mansour, the old levelheaded warrior who effortlessly guides the troupe, letting himself be borne along by the natural flow of their progression. Samuel's conversation with him about the mountains of Lebanon and the tribes of the Sudan seem to occupy the man more than setting their course, which seems to take care of itself. But he falls respectfully silent when Samuel stops talking and becomes absorbed in the astonishing beauty of the great tapering rocks, the abrupt pink mountains, and the horizon suddenly disclosing arid panoramas and crenelated summits. The first night, they stop at the oasis of Bayda; the second, in a valley hollowed out by recent rains, where water still pools in the holes and fissures. That night, around the fire, Ibn Mansour tells of the Bani Ayyad, tribes he knows, and promises to introduce Samuel to their chieftains. Then they talk of genealogies, of onomastics, and Samuel tells the tale of that poor Lebanese emigrant to England who, in order to be left alone, decided one day to make his name more English-sounding, and so from Mr. Sawwan became Mr. Shawn, not suspecting that at the same time in Edinburgh, Scotland, the final offspring of a very ancient and prestigious lineage by the name of Shawn, lay dying. And this final offspring, doubtless something of a prankster, had asked that his millions and his entire family inheritance be given to works of charity unless a Shawn could be found living somewhere in the world, to whom he would then bequeath all his worldly goods. And as fate would have it, Samuel went on, in a few weeks the little Lebanese emigrant, not understanding why in the slightest, became the trustee of a fortune whose ancestry was not his own, from then on living like a squatter in castles and spending the annuities from countless properties he'd never even heard of a few years ago. When Samuel was done, the Egyptian corporal sitting with the group by the fire declared that he, on the other hand, actually was descended from a very ancient family, that of Rameses II. He is asked if his name is Rameses, or something like it, but he answers no, his name is Mohammed Ahmed like every other Egyptian, and he laughs. His audience laughs with him, and he explains that if those cordially gathered would please follow his reasoning, and supposing that three thousand years ago, Rameses had one hundred children as they claim, and each of these children had at least, say, ten apiece of their own, well, if those cordially gathered did the math, multiplying all this by the hundreds, even thousands of generations from then till now, there was a good chance that any old Egyptian could trace his ancestry, at one time or another, to a descendant of Rameses, and therefore to Rameses himself.

When he is done, he looks amused; he is heavily built and even a bit broad in the beam, and seems always passably cheery. Poking at the fire, he waits while his companions do their calculations. Samuel studies him discreetly and takes a spontaneous liking to him. Ibn Mansour nods, reckoning that all this is well and good, as does Fahim el Mawlud. Only the British sergeant remains stone-faced, even after Samuel politely translates the entire conversation for him. But right from the start, this sergeant has seemed such a well brought-up boy that never does the slightest hint of remonstration about a single thing—the heat, the humidity, the flies—allow itself to be glimpsed on his face with its stiff little mustache, such that Samuel finally wonders if it's phlegm, impassivity, or indifference, but right now, he thinks it must be a kind of contempt, such that in this man's eyes nothing is worth wasting the time for so much as a grimace. And surely it is this hint of contempt, but also a hidden shyness, that explain why during the short halts, instead of making straight for the shade of a rock, a tamarind tree, or the sheets that have been spread out, as everyone else does, the sergeant pretends to busy himself with his two camels carrying explosives, gelatin, and detonators, until Hamid Ibn Mansour or Samuel call him over, and then he comes, rigid and upright, and sits down without a word.

On the morning of the third day, on a broad plain dotted with spiny thickets and a few short acacias, the railway line of Al-Hejaz finally appears in the middle of the desert, offered up defenselessly, lined at regular intervals by telegraph poles. It's too tempting and almost too easy; the little troupe takes every liberty it wants to with the tracks, blowing up the rails, uprooting poles, rejoicing at a gallop down this strip of desert in enemy territory, then vanishing inland into the mountains to the east after the caravan which has taken the lead and is heading north, toward Bir Suheila. A few hours later, Rosemond turns up behind a hill with two Bedouins, head wrapped up in an Arab keffiyeh, uniform unkempt, and in his company, Samuel makes for the camp of the Bani Suheila, where Rosemond is confronted with a tough problem. On the way, he relates that, contrary to the rumors that have reached Al-Wajh, the Bani Suheila have indeed helped him in his initiatives against the railway, and a week earlier, they derailed a train carrying forty families of deportees from the region around

Medina. Rosemond managed to keep the Bani Suheila from slaughtering them along with the Turkish soldiers and ransacking all their belongings. Still, the Bani Suheila took at least some of what little goods they had, in exchange for sparing their lives. Since that day, thanks to Rosemond's intercession, the deportees, who are clearly with Faisal, have been welcomed at the nomads' camp, though the latter are enraged, short of water, and above all, covetous of what personal effects the deportees retain. In a nutshell, everyone is staring daggers at one another, and as a result Rosemond himself can no longer carry out his missions from fear that a massacre will occur in his absence. After an hour, as Rosemond is talking, the camp of the Bani Suheila appears.

It is enormous, as camps go, because it is made up of two halves. That of the tribe itself, with its tents around a few wells, and that of the deportees, a wretched circle of sheets hung up between scraggly trees. Askar Chalabi el Suheili, chief of the Bani Suheila, greets Samuel and Hamid Ibn Mansour el Hawli with displays of joy, and as night is falling he invites them to dinner, along with three main worthies from among the deportees. There is also a strange fellow, a Frenchman with a shy look about him, who is among the rescued deportees and who, ever since the attack on the train, has been waiting for a solution to all this business to be found. Being here seems to distress him, and no one understands his presence, because no one, absolutely no one, speaks French: not the Bedouins, or the people of Medina, or even Rosemond. But Samuel does, and he has a brief conversation with the Frenchman, whose name is Vincent d'Argès, and who says he was part of Jossin and Savignac's archeological mission to Arabia at the beginning of the war. When the Ottoman Empire entered the conflict, the Turks arrested him and forced him to write a report on the state of archeology in the region, and then deported him for internment. Samuel translates the Frenchman's words as he speaks. Everyone listens and remains pensive while the rice is brought out and the meal begins. The firelight around which the gathering dines has abolished the vast magnificence that the firmament unfurls over the desert. The density of the night seems almost as imposing to Samuel as the nature on which it has shut like a lid. The atmosphere is somewhat tense, the worthies from Medina, visibly ill at ease, venturing only polite phrases and invocations, and the Frenchman, after his conversation with Samuel, has fallen silent and eats discreetly, a small pouch of sorts wedged between his legs. Askar Chalabi el Suheili, however, is interested in Samuel, and wants to know why a Bani Ayyad has a Christian, even Jewish first name, and Samuel tells him that it's probably because he belongs to a Christian Bani Ayyad tribe. This sets the chief thinking; the worthies from Medina adopt a somber air, for to them all this seems to add to the complexity of things, of the world, and so, to ease the atmosphere a bit, people begin telling funny stories and, laughing, reach out their hands for the platters of oily rice covered in the meat of goats and sheep.

The next day, in the rediscovered splendor of the world, beneath the great rocky peak like a skyward-pointing finger where the Bani Suheila make their camp, Samuel opens the talks. After half a day, things are clear. The worthies from Medina, unable to go home, declare that they wish to go to Mecca. They are highly uneasy around Samuel, who realizes this is because he's a Christian. But the old Arabic he learned from his father, earthy and colorful, serves him well on this occasion. He employs it joyously, and the admiring Medinans end up becoming more obliging. Nevertheless, they have made their decision: if they must go somewhere, then to Mecca they shall go. Or to Medina, if the war is over by the time they get there. They refuse all suggestion of Al-Wajh, which is much closer but, being in no position to impose their views, they finally agree to the idea of going to Yanbu and, from there, sailing to Jeddah, the port serving the holy city. As Rosemond is of the opinion that whatever is done, the Bani Suheila must not be asked to escort the deportees, even to the borders of their own territory, and as Askar Chalabi el Suheili will for his part agree to sell only fifteen camels, which, to put it bluntly, does no good at all, Samuel finds himself in quite an awkward position. For camels he does have, and enough to pull off the job in a pinch, if everyone squeezes in a little, so Hamid's twenty-odd men can protect the deportees.

In the end, he takes Fahim el Mawlud aside and, under an acacia, tells him they're going to have to change course for a moment, head south, and above all, change cargo, leaving the palace here and taking on the Medinans. Mawlud is displeased, less about changing the route than having to haul humans, that doesn't seem like a good idea at all, and will considerably lengthen the journey's duration as initially predicted. Mawlud is someone with a very proud look about him, but wily of eye, who at the drop of a hat will forget his princely bearing to come begging a favor. And now at the drop of this hat, he starts out prideful, fingering his prayer beads with calm and dignity, playing the malcontent, the man given something to worry about, frowning with a preoccupied air and then, when Samuel starts offering attractive sums of gold, he begins to wriggle, pockets his prayer beads in his robe, and engages in a little rascally haggling. To be done with it, Samuel gives him what he wants, and wins him over effortlessly. That evening, he gathers the Medinan worthies and the Bani Suheila chieftains and, in the presence of Rosemond, Hamid Ibn Mansour el Hawli, Mawlud, and the Frenchman, announces that the deportees will be leaving first thing in the morning, in his care, escorted by his own troops, on the camels of his own caravan. For the first time, it is clearly evident that everything the caravan is carrying belongs to Samuel, and no one makes any comments, for they recognize that he has just made a significant sacrifice, and respect him for doing so. For his part, Samuel thinks he is about to render unto Faisal and his cause, the English cause, what Moore has given him in their name. Before giving his final consent, Askar Chalabi el Suheili demands from the Medinans one final compensation for his trouble. They assure him, as they already have a hundred times, that what little they still possess is all they have left of their entire lives, that when they return home, their houses will doubtless have been destroyed, but they agree to take up a small collection. Samuel takes this a step further, announcing that he will pay another three hundred sovereigns for all the deportees together, including children and the Frenchman, and he will leave the rifles. The agreement having been struck, Samuel then has a private conversation with Chalabi el Suheili, whom he asks the favor of guarding his palace. He knows this is like entrusting a chest of jewels to a kleptomaniac, but in payment for this singular custodianship he offers gold, always gold, and promises more gold still upon his return, should his property remain untouched, and Chalabi agrees.

*

An hour later, the Frenchman comes to Samuel's tent to thank him for buying his freedom, and Samuel bursts out laughing. "You weren't being held for ransom," he says, and Vincent d'Argès smiles, looking embarrassed. He is sitting cross-legged, facing Samuel, and doesn't know what to say. So to liven up this tête-à-tête, Samuel asks him where he wishes to go. D'Argès replies that he will go to Jeddah, and from there to Egypt, then Europe. It occurs to Samuel at this point that there is a question he is not asking: he is wondering how this poor boy will manage to finance such a trip. But the query must be written all over his face, for d'Argès smiles that smile of his which has the gift of spontaneously lighting up his face like a child's. In fact, Samuel wonders if he is not actually a child. He can't be very old, Samuel thinks, his gauntness has given him no wrinkles nor has it aged him. As he considers this, discreetly studying the Frenchman, the latter's smile fades but his expression remains luminous. He removes the strange and very-heaving looking satchel he wears slung across his chest, sets it down like a goatskin bladder between himself and Samuel, opens it, and after plunging both hands inside as if into a bag of gold, comes out with a head, a severed head—not a real head, but the wondrous head of a god, or rather a goddess, sculpted from reddish stone, eyes wide open, a hint of a smile on her lips, curly hair like that of Arabs from the peninsula held back by a band in the Greek style, the head of a Hellenized statue which in one fell swoop alters the atmosphere inside the tent, concentrates and heightens the air, the shapes and colors around it. Before Samuel's astonished eyes, d'Argès smiles once more and reminds Samuel that he is an archaeologist. He explains that this head comes from the region around Mada'in

Saleh, and belongs to the goddess Allat, or Al-'Uzzá, or Atargatis—that is, one of the goddesses the Nabataeans and the Ghassanids worshipped, that there were many such heads in the same region, but that place is now inaccessible to him. This head is worth a great deal, a great deal indeed, and he offers it to Samuel in repayment for the ransom (he smiles at this word), and for some money to get home to Europe. Let us speak no more of the ransom, Samuel assures him; moreover, it was not he who paid but His Majesty's Treasury, and as for the rest, everything will work out, there is no need to sacrifice such a magnificent object.

8

IT IS A LONG PROCESSION OF BEGGARS THAT LEAVES THE Bani Suheila encampment. And yet none of these people began as beggars; they are mostly the families of dignitaries, merchants, well-to-do tradesmen, carpenters. and coppersmiths as well as a few shopkeepers—families of wealth and small industry that Fakhri Pasha, governor of Medina, has accused of sympathizing with the Arab Revolt. All these people now form a great convoy of outcasts, trying as best they can to cling to some noble bearing, the most prominent seated on camels, their wives in improvised palanquins, their black slaves and their children riding mules that once bore rifles. The rest share what animals remain or go on foot, and all this stretches out over more than a mile, scantily escorted by Ibn Mansour's twenty Bedouins, before whom the prospect of gold was dangled, gold that Samuel Ayyad still carries and always will. He has divvied up the bags between himself and Mohammed Ahmed, the Egyptian corporal who has become his confidant, whom he sometimes accidentally calls Gawad, and whose three fellow countrymen have also come along, with the reassuring machine gun everyone knows will be no good if they are ambushed. Samuel rides beside Hamid, and next to him are Mohammed Ahmed, Fahim el Mawlud, and the explosives sergeant who every now and again lets the Frenchman ride behind him—the Frenchman who, goddess head slung across his chest, barely says a thing, except when Samuel tosses a friendly word his way to ease his loneliness, whereupon his timidity gives way to a lively, laughing look.

For weeks they advance this way in a southwesterly direction. Then one morning, as a general might review the procession of his tired troops, Samuel watches the slow stream of repatriates pass before him, crossing the railroad tracks. His companions quiver with impatience—the train could come at any moment. But the tracks remain completely deserted, left to themselves. Afterward, the caravan veers truer south, surrounded by blazing summits, across a landscape furnished on all sides with great domes of rock and outpourings of sculptural shapes the dazzling light keeps them from seeing clearly, as if their beauty were such that no gaze could linger on them, for fear of searing the eye. During these endless days, it occurs to Samuel that he was once on his way home and is now instead helping others make their way home, a kind of unwitting Moses leading his Hebrews back to their promised land. And at times, he thinks, this is what the people of Israel must have looked like wandering in the Sinai, swaying clusters of men on cam-

elback, clinging to their mounts like castaways to flotsam, mysterious women being led along in palanquins
with draperies aflutter or simply veiled, upright, like
black candlesticks on their mounts, men on foot, bags
slung this way and that, faces vanishing beneath heaped
rags that are their only headdress, and also slaves riding
sidesaddle on mules laden with bundles, crockery, and
rugs, all scattered and dangerously strung out, defended
by a few dozen warriors, lighter and more mobile but
just as sapped by the heat and harsh light. The only dif-
ference, he reflects at last, is that the Hebrews were not
transporting a god in a satchel, and he wonders what
the Medinans, just as fiercely attached to the idea of the
unrepresentable divine as the Jews, would think of the
singular baggage the Frenchman is lugging along among
them, were they to learn of it.

And in this story, Pharaoh, too, has his counter-
part—the bands of Billi or Shammar plunderers raiding
far afield, harassing the caravan. For the unusual cortege and the prayer rugs it carries, the plain crockery for
ablutions, the purported jewels of the dignitaries' wives
but also their black slaves, soon attract the far-flung and
mysterious people of the desert. Attacks are so greatly
dreaded as to sow constant panic up and down the convoy. One morning, everyone points out tall pillars of
smoke rising from the earth, upright and unmoving as
those of Abel's sacrifices. But these fires are too distant
to belong to possible pursuers. One afternoon, the rear-

guard turns up in a fever of excitement, proclaiming riders, many riders, an hour away. Yet these prove to be but phantasms the warriors thought to see in the desert's mirages, in the blaze of the earth when it seems to touch the sky, for in fact through his binoculars Samuel sees nothing of these legions of soldiers except sunstruck crimson valleys, stony sculptures frozen like Lot's daughters and, along the horizon, lunar mountains, red and black, and he can almost hear the eternal silence of these infinite spaces.

However, very soon the attacks become real. They are furtive, and the plunderers elusive. One day, three strapping young men sitting in the shade of a rock are found dead, naked, stripped even of their underthings, sandals in shreds. One morning, an attack zeroes in on a group in the middle, when the long procession has begun to fray. The men put up a fight, the women in their black robes ebb and flow from the tide of the assault, and finally, the Howeitat come to the rescue with Samuel and Hamid. Shots ring out and the attackers flee, leaving behind on the ground two of their own and a wounded camel that is finished off and served up that very night for dinner, in the middle of a camp pitched near a few brackish watering holes. The camel is in fact a windfall, for food is scarce. Now and again, a few of Hamid's Bedouins go hunting. They disappear for whole days, worrying the others, then return with ostriches, oryxes, and once, a gazelle. All this improves their day-to-day existence, otherwise supplemented by goat meat Samuel buys from poor, peaceful nomad families they encounter along the way. And then one day, the hunters return overjoyed, carrying three live monkeys bound to poles, much to everyone's delight. These are set aside for a time when hunger may grow too strong; meanwhile, they are a source of amusement. A woodworker builds them makeshift cages of tamarind wood. Mockeries of clothing are sewn for them, skirts and robes; beribboned *agals* are set on their heads. They become everyone's favorite entertainment and during stops are teased, made to dance, left to pull their funny faces, their peculiar little expressions in which one and all find the distortion of their own image, and Samuel, as a graduate of the Syrian Protestant College of Beirut, where Darwin's theories are making waves, declares to the Frenchman one day that the caravan is now transporting the entire evolutionary ladder: monkeys, humans—themselves divided into free men and slaves—and a deity in a satchel.

But the attacks continue, and one morning, Hamid declares that they must make contact with the Billi chieftains, to whom the wells in these mountains belong, as they are masters of the routes and could provide a guarantee of safety against the raids. "What chieftains?" Samuel asks. Hamid speaks of Nawaf Abu Shaddad, a powerful sheikh in the region. He adds that he doesn't like the man much, that he's too obsequious and lacking in generosity, but he could keep the bands of plunderers away. However, information on him is hazy. His favorite residence is the oasis of Al Arozz, but the nomad families met along the way claim he is currently by the Mukhlis wells, where Samuel's troupe is going. Samuel decides to ride ahead, flying Faisal's banners high. However, there is no sign of Nawaf. The Mukhlis wells are deserted, water is abundant there and fairly beautiful amidst a few pretty clusters of palm trees. That night, the repatriates make their camp there. According to what has become a habit, Samuel's tents, the Egyptians', and the Howeitats' are left to the women. As these aren't enough, long screens of sheets and other fabrics are hung from hedges, and the camp begins to resemble the bivouacs of bohemian vagrants. The men eat by the fires and tell each other stories, there is laughter, even the Medinans have recovered some cheer, fun is had with the monkeys' clowning, songs are sung, and then the Howeitat dance beneath the great gemstones of the night sky. The next day, no one wants to leave, so great is their exhaustion, so beneficent the shade of the trees, and so sweet the water. A few noble ladies make themselves comfortable on rugs, and their slaves bring them drinks in ewers; everyone imitates them, and the oasis turns into a giant picnic spilling over onto the nearby rocks. The Egyptian soldiers, lying on their sides and backs, indulge in long naps in the shade next to their machine gun. The Frenchman seems to drift off into daydreams with his back against a tree and the head of his god between his legs. In the middle of all this, Hamid is worried, very worried, and he finally passes his worry on to Samuel. For one cannot take one's ease in such a fashion at these wells, not without their owner's approval. In the early afternoon, Samuel manages to get the caravan ready for departure. But it is too late. Just when they are ready, a Bedouin of Hamid's comes galloping up to announce a significant party to the north, and indeed, Nawaf Abu Shaddad soon appears.

*

He towers atop his glittering camel bedecked like a wedding tent. His pearl-encrusted silver dagger seems a toy against his belly, his brocaded robe and damasked keffiyeh accentuate his imposing head with his prying eyes and fleshy lips. Accompanying him are a hundred-odd warriors, and he declares that he is unhappy with the liberties that have been taken with his wells, water is scarce, he will require compensation. Hamid tries to make him understand, but Nawaf, without dismounting, addresses him familiarly, and Hamid takes umbrage. The negotiations are about to get out of hand when Samuel intervenes and asks to speak among friends, for the Billi are Faisal's allies, and the caravan consists of people also loyal to the prince. At the sight of this man who speaks Arabic but looks like an Englishman, with his military attire, wily eyes, and European mustache under his agal, Nawaf agrees to dismount. Drawing him aside, Samuel offers him two hundred gold pieces for his troubles. Nawaf, a giant of a man gone slightly soft, rolls his eyes and begins to laugh, his belly shaking beneath his enormous robe. He shoots quietly ironic glances at his companions, who return wide conniving grins full of suggestion, and then he declares that he doesn't want gold, the Turks and Faisal have showered him with more gold than he can hide or spend; he wants gifts in kind. And when Samuel shows him, with a gesture, the pitiful state of his flock, Nawaf shrugs. "If you have nothing," says he, "then give me a woman."

By way of reply, Samuel gives the order to make camp again, then has the machine gun set up between the rocks, its muzzle pointed right where Nawaf Abu Shaddad is pitching his own tents. After which, at his request, the explosives sergeant readies odd-looking bags of small mines made from dynamite and detonators that Samuel then positions around the Billi camp. When evening comes, he sends a messenger to Nawaf saying that his request has been denied, and that two hundred gold sovereigns, a fair compensation, remain at his disposal as previously offered. Nawaf's answer is brief: there must be a woman with the gold. The next day, Samuel heads for Nawaf's camp with the British sergeant and Mohammed Ahmed to negotiate once more. The Billi chieftain listens to him and watches with eyes that lie in wait behind plump cheeks. Then he shifts, straightens, lifts the elbow propped on his rug. An odd moment of chaos, and the white mountain resettles; Abu Shaddad is sitting up. He neatens his robe, mutters imprecations, and suddenly his eyes grow rounder, almost affable, his mood brightens, and he speaks. But only in order to return stubbornly to the same idea: he will accept the gold, but requires a woman as tribute (and this time, as if to complicate matters, he uses the word "female" in contempt), or else he will slaughter all the water thieves. When he falls silent, Samuel catches a brief glint in his eye, a glint of great mirth, of boundless joy that vanishes quite quickly, and for Samuel, it is as if he has espied, through a crack in the door at an old wise man's house, a scene of witchery and mischief. Samuel is suddenly convinced that Nawaf Abu Shaddad has made all this fuss for his own amusement, a bit of entertainment while terrifying the caravan.

For the rest of the afternoon, the mood at the Medinan camp is somber. The dignitaries and Samuel's companions have any number of ideas: flee, charge into Nawaf's camp with the machine gun. Fahim suggests sending a slave woman as tribute, or even two, to equal a free woman, and Mohammed Ahmed laughingly proposes offering him the machine gun, since that thing has to be pampered like a woman, and rubbed, and mounted and dismounted, but Nawaf couldn't manage it, so what's the point? Everyone looks at the Egyptian corporal reproachfully—how can he joke at a time like this?—but once again, Samuel gazes at him admiringly, for not only does he like the man's sense of humor, but the corporal's just given him an idea to boot, and he asks that they leave things to him. In the hours that follow, Samuel recovers his playful cheer—"You want to have some fun, Nawaf Abu Shaddad? Well, I'll give you something to laugh about!" he says, almost aloud—and he also reflects that he'd never have believed the strange whims and madness of the Lebanese explorer in Dar Tama would be of use to him someday. He thinks back, almost moved, and two hours later a small convoy of three camels, one bearing a palanquin, leaves the Medinan camp for that of Abu Shaddad. At Nawaf's camp, there is much commotion and cries that tribute has been paid. Nawaf is astounded and intrigued. He is in his tent, wearing an agal with silken gold cords that lend his childish face and ogre-like size something grotesque, and he announces greedily that he is ready to receive his gift. But soon quite a ruckus breaks out, along with imprecations and cries of vengeance, there is a mad rush for Nawaf's tent, and he himself comes out at last to see what's going on, only to discover that inside the palanquin the Lebanese with the face of an Englishman has sent is no woman, but a cage, and inside the cage, a female monkey dolled up in a ridiculous dress, outrageously festooned with bracelets and necklaces, a monkey that abruptly begins to fidget and whine, excited by the commotion the sight of her has stirred among the humans. When Nawaf turns to the leader of the Medinan delegation—none other than Mohammed Ahmed—he hears the declaration that, of all the females they asked, this was the only one who did not refuse to offer herself up.

Nawaf Abu Shaddad appreciates a good jest, but this one costs him dearly. For afterward, he is forced to avenge his honor. But the caravan has left. It hasn't gone far yet when he sends his Bedouins in pursuit, but no sooner do they ride out, than the Egyptians' machine gun speaks from the rocks where it is hiding, it speaks again, incessantly, and the echo of its great coughing voice reaches the ears of the repatriates as Nawaf's warriors fall back in panic and one of their horses tramples one of the sergeant's mines, which explodes in an upheaval of sand and bits of camel. The muffled noise informs the Medinans, who are an hour away, that things are going rather well. Nawaf isn't laughing anymore, and Samuel soon catches up to his convoy along with the Egyptians, the sergeant, and the Howeitat who stayed behind with him. For two days, they are on the alert, sleeping little, moving as fast as they can to leave Bani Shaddad territory behind, which Hamid believes they have done by nightfall on the third day, upon reaching the wells at Bir Allaya. After that, the reputation of the machine gun and the mines seems to keep plunderers and Nawaf's kin at a distance, and they make their way unmolested past mountains and valleys, through the heart of granite deserts whose peaks glow red like crowns in the setting sun.

Amidst these difficult splendors, the caravan drags its rags along, its camels are encumbered, the men's heads are wrapped in pitiful heaps of scraps. The camps are vast and disorderly, strewn across the face of the earth, and during the night, women emerge cautiously from their tents, take a few steps with their faces bare before God, then lift their robes and piss beneath the great jewelry chest of the heavens.

*

For days on end, they make their way south in this fashion, but it is as if they are getting nowhere, so greatly do the mountains and the valleys and then the escarpments come to resemble one another. And yet they push on. Soon, near the mountains of Al Jarf, Samuel steers the convoy west. He is starting to feel impatience eating away at him; he fears Chalabi el Suheili will use his long absence to have his way with the palace. In his disheveled corporal's uniform from the Egyptian army, Mohammed Ahmed is the only one to interpret Samuel's often somber mood correctly, and he offers to return to Bir Suheila with two or three Bedouins to guard the goods. Samuel refuses, of course, for he hopes they will soon reach Yanbu. And in fact, they are nearing the small coastal town. But meanwhile, the troubles keep coming. One day, the caravaners want a raise, on another, the Howeitat are about to mutiny because they've had only one chance at plundering. And then one morning, Hamid threatens to leave with his men, and no one quite understands the reason for his falling out. He has had words with a Medinan dignitary to whom he pointed out, at dawn before departure, that the direction of the man's prayer was slightly off-true with respect to the holy city. The Medinan took this for irony, sharp words were exchanged, and the Medinan finally said the last thing he needed was a Bedouin to teach him devotion, and now here is Hamid, threatening to drop everything and go home. The other Medinan worthies conduct an attempt at reconciliation at the foot of a cliff that bounces people's words back as echoes whenever they raise their voices even a tad, forcing them to speak in low tones in a stark reminder of mutual respect. This is in fact a handy argument the mediators between Hamid and the dignitary use: be humble, be ashamed, don't grow angry over a trifle when the power of Allah is manifest everywhere around you. At last the two men admit they've behaved like children; everyone gathers for tea, joking and laughing, then resumes their journey, and the next day, things take a slight turn: it is the Frenchman who opens up to Samuel.

He does so at night, when the camp is quiet. By the light of one last fire, he keeps vigil with Samuel, Hamid, Mohammed Ahmed, and two Medinan worthies. With his exquisite courtesy, as if he were timidly waiting for everyone else to finish talking before speaking in turn, he opens his mouth only after a long silence. He turns to Samuel, naturally, and declares that, now that they are no longer very far from Yanbu, there is something he would like to *confide*. Samuel, who speaks French fairly well, initially has no doubt as to the verb's meaning, he thinks Vincent d'Argès is about to tell him a secret. The fire unfurls its pantomime with long reddish beckonings, leaps, and cracklings, and d'Argès confesses that at several points over the last few months, especially when they were in the Jabal Jafr, he considered leaving the caravan and striking out alone for Mada'in Saleh, where he had been working before his arrest. "I thought it over, I thought it over a great deal," says he, staring fixedly at the dancing flame. "But in the end, I gave up on the idea. Still, I left a great many gods and goddesses there, sleeping in the sand." At these strange words, Samuel, who has stopped raking over bits of wood at the heart of the flames, watches him attentively. The Frenchman falls silent for a moment. His face is candid and serene as ever, even in the glow from the flames. The others gathered take his silence as an opportunity to get up, since the conversation is now in a language they don't understand and they will get nothing from it. They murmur their good nights and when they have, one by one, all vanished into the dark, d'Argès tells Samuel it is these gods and goddesses that he wishes to confide to Samuel. And he says that in the region of Raghed, near the royal tombs of Mada'in, is a place called the Son-in-Law's Head, and he pronounces the name in Ara-

bic—Ras es Sohr. It is a rocky outcrop the local Arabs
know well. But no doubt Hamid's Howeitat know it,
too. "They will help you find it," he says. "And if they
cannot, the Bani Harf will. For the wells in the region
are theirs, as is Ras es Sohr. In a cave high up the west
flank of this rock, I myself have hidden statues of gods
from ancient desert kingdoms, vowing I would someday return for them." Then he falls silent once more.
The wood pops in the fire, a spark flies up and falls like
a shooting star onto his worn pants. Instinctively running a hand over the ruined cloth, he says, "But I will
never go there again. I've had enough. I am weary of all
this. So do it for me, Monsieur Ayyad. No one but you
deserves to discover these wonders. I confide in you this
task." Samuel reminds him that he himself is soon leaving for Bir Suheila, and d'Argès could join him. They
would journey to Mada'in Saleh together. "I am weary
of this country and everything that has befallen me,"
d'Argès repeats. "I no longer have the strength to roam
the desert. I must go home to Europe. I leave you these
treasures, treat them as I would have." Smiling, Samuel
asks him how he managed to work and hide the gods
in the Arabian soil while speaking nothing but French.
After a moment of silence, d'Argès says that it is a long
story. Samuel waits, but the Frenchman says nothing
more. For a moment, the two men remain silent, face-
to-face. The fire is now but a firmament of red dots in
the dark night of charred wood. Above, the other fir-

mament suddenly comes to life, crisscrossed by fleeting sparks. Samuel rises, and to the Frenchman it seems he will touch the Milky Way with his brow. But Samuel says, in closing, "I thank you for your friendship. I will try to find these gods sleeping in the desert."

9

SAMUEL DOES NOT ENTER THE TOWN OF YANBU BECAUSE
he cannot wait to turn back, and what's more, he has
no wish to be in touch with the British military hierarchy again. His mission is over and, all that remains
for him to do now is, as Moore said, slip away. When
the small town appears on the coast, he asks the repatriates and Vincent d'Argès to finish their journey on
foot, escorted by the English sergeant and Mohammed
Ahmed, who sheds a tear at parting ways with him. He
also entrusts them with what remains of the gold he was
given in Al-Wajh, then lets the camels rest for a day and
a night in the hills before heading back the way he came,
despite bitter remonstrations from the caravaners, who
feel they have earned a rest in Yanbu. Afterward, with
no cargo, the journey goes infinitely faster. Hamid and
Fahim el Mawlud ride beside him, as well as the twenty
Howeitat he has remunerated with his own gold, the
gold he carries with him everywhere, which he is bringing home to Lebanon to enrich his family and provide
for his sisters' dowry. The crossing that took months out-
bound now takes only two weeks, after which, instead

of heading for Bir Suheila, Samuel makes a detour and heads for Mada'in Saleh. For several days, his empty caravan advances through valleys thick with limestone pachyderms or whole fields of crooked stalagmites that leave them feeling like they've crossed through a swirling crowd of mad dancers and wild bacchantes. This vast landscape is sweltering in the violent light of day but dawn softens its contours, dusk clads them in hyacinth, crimson, and gold, and suddenly the desert resembles the set of a lavish opera.

One morning, the troupe finally reaches the ancient city of the Nabataeans and its rows of tombs dug into the rock, a fantastical dormitory for the eternal repose of the princes of the desert. The next day, one of Hamid's men guides them to Ras es Sohr. The oasis is a small palm grove in the armpit of a great, round, and perfectly bald rock. On the west flank, erosion has carved a small formation, a play of curves like the cambered pleat of a folded curtain. And high up, in fact, in the fold itself, grows a thorny thicket. Samuel scales the crack, followed by his companions, who laugh at this unexpected game. Prey to an entire range of sensations—breathless, heart beating, feverish, open to all manner of aesthetic wonder—he comes upon the cave. He pushes through the thorny shrubs, getting viciously scratched, penetrates the gloom almost on all fours, and like the archeologist realizing that looters have beaten him to Pharaoh's tomb, he finds there is nothing in the cavern—not gods, goddesses, or anything else. Just scraps of rags that have almost moldered into the sand.

"I expected as much," he keeps saying to Hamid and Fahim a bit later, sitting under the trees. "But still—to abscond with everything in the cave, someone had to know it was there."

"The Bani Harf must have stolen the treasure," says Hamid. "There's no other explanation."

"Then let us go ask them," Samuel suggests.

*

The next day, the patriarch of a group of Harfi whose clan is camped out nearby—a skinny, toothless old man with a carefully groomed goatee and a sparrow hawk's eyes—listens with a knowing and compassionate air as Samuel speaks of Vincent d'Argès. He nods and mumbles that of course the Bani Harf knew the Frenchman: quite a character, with many strange ideas. When Samuel wants to know more, the chieftain gives a vague wave of his hand. However, when it comes to the vanished treasure, he is fairly precise. According to him, the thief is most certainly Raeed Hussein el Harfi, a powerful Bani Harf chieftain who once helped the Frenchman with his excavations but sold him to the Turks. "But," Samuel asks, "wasn't d'Argès part of the group with the priests Savignac and Jossin?" The patriarch adjusts the sides of his headdress, and then (as if he needed to look presentable in order to be surprised) widens his eyes uncomprehendingly. Samuel repeats himself, and the chieftain laughingly declares, not at all, d'Argès (which he pronounces as *Darjis*, the tonic accent weighing down the second syllable of the word) was alone, by God, utterly and completely alone. Two days later, another Bani Harf chieftain confirms the likely connection between Raeed Hussein el Harfi and the disappearance of the gods, and with another question of Samuel's, takes his time, breaks a few twigs as if in preparation for that night's fire, and finally says that d'Argès was an odd man with odd dreams. Then, as if to conclude the meeting, he repeats pensively that at any rate, it was Raeed Hussein el Harfi, that coward, who sold him to the Turks.

To find this Raeed Hussein el Harfi, the powerful chieftain who smaller clans claim possesses several hundred warriors, Samuel heads north, which is at any rate the direction of Bir Suheila, and as luck would have it, he winds up crossing paths with the disloyal chieftain's very own son, Zeid Ibn Raeed. This happens one morning when riders are reported to the east. Zeid is not with his tribe, but he is bringing back camels from pasture, and he falls in with Samuel after Samuel declares his wish to meet his father, the famous Sheikh Raeed. This Zeid is a slender, handsome boy with perfectly shaped eyebrows, luscious lips, stunning white teeth, and a broad smile. Like a a piece of sculpture from antiquity, Samuel thinks, and fairly quickly decides to tackle the question of d'Argès, no matter the resulting mess, huffiness, anger, or feigned ignorance. Though nothing of the sort ensues, what happens is more pernicious still. Zeid is not surprised when Samuel utters the name d'Argès. He acknowledges that the Frenchman spent time with his tribe, that they helped him with his work, but of course, on the subject of the gods he was to have hidden at the oasis of Ras es Sohr, Zeid knows absolutely nothing. It's probably a pure fabrication. All this he says in snatches, in a restless way that lends little credence, for Zeid is elusive as water, answering only in hints and allusions. It is very difficult to tell just what he knows; in his robe and keffiyeh with its thin cords of gold brocade he keeps darting forward on his camel, certain members of his entourage following suit, and then coming back to the group at a trot, as if to flaunt his enthusiasm, his impetuosity, and also his impatience, or else the beauty of his mount. Unless he is seeking to seduce one or another of Samuel's warriors, at whom he glances with interest, or Samuel himself, whom he has asked ten times over if he will agree to sell his russet camel cow.

Between two spirited bursts of speed on Zeid's part, Samuel manages to find a way back to his subject and get a more or less complete answer when he asks how d'Argès got any work done in the region speaking only French. "What do you mean, only French?" asks Zeid, laughing wholeheartedly. "He spoke better Arabic than you and I, and Turkish, too!" After which, as if this absurd question has just put an end to any seriousness in a conversation barely begun, making the rest of it pointless, off he shoots like an arrow, shouting right and left, carried away by enthusiasm, by unrestrained jubilation, and is soon joined by a few of Hamid's Howeitat, for whom a call to race is irresistible, and so it goes for the whole rest of the day, across this vast empty landscape interrupted now and again by monumental domes of rock, stone dinosaurs, acropolises in the middle of nowhere. That night, they stop at a small oasis whose wells belong to Zeid's family. He makes himself at home among the blessed flora, strolling about like Adam in Eden; no doubt he would gladly lead one of Hamid's warriors down the garden path: in the night, he struts, he boasts, he jests, he flits about, gaze fluttering from one man to the next, goes from fire to fire and proposes a flame-jumping contest. The warriors and caravaners have made him one of their own, and laugh at his jokes, but he is beginning to irritate Samuel. During the evening, Zeid suggests a game of heads or tails to those gathered and pulls a coin from a pocket of his robe, which he's hitched up to his belt. Heads, he calls, tosses the majidi which spins in the air, leaving the circle of light, and returning; he catches it, and goes from guest to guest showing them the result, until he reaches Samuel. Then, with a bit of legerdemain he deliberately lets only Samuel glimpse, he swaps for the Turkish coin another he tosses up and snatches from midair with his right hand, and what he now presents to the Lebanese man on the back of his left hand, with an air about him that is keen, focused, worried, and laughing all at once, is no longer Ottoman currency, or English, or French, or Egyptian, but an ancient coin, a beautiful coin from the time of the Nabataeans, with slightly battered sides, a laurel-crowned king in delicate profile ringed by Greek letters, and afterward Samuel will no longer remember if what struck him at the time was the king's almond-shaped eye on the coin or Zeid's, staring at him in triumph.

At any rate, as soon as he's sure Samuel's gotten the message, Zeid continues his game with the others. But Samuel takes it calmly. He refuses to concede the point, certain that if he did so, Zeid would go back to playing the spoiled child who knows he is indispensable and takes advantage of one's patience. He does not speak to Zeid before going to bed, and when they set out again the next morning, he behaves as if the boy did not exist. He no longer asks him any questions, losing all interest in him and leaving him to race off suddenly on mad stampedes. And so it is Zeid who, around midmorning, comes to tell Samuel that if he wishes, Zeid will guide him to Bir Hamed (and he points at the horizon to his left, where the desert looks the same as ever, unto infinity) where (so he claims) Sheikh Fayed Ibn Alaeddine el Talleati, the man who sold Darjis to the Turks, makes his camp this time of year. Zeid seems sure of the effect his words will have, but Samuel looks him straight in the eye and remarks that, really, in this part of the desert, everyone seems to know d'Argès, everyone has helped him, and everyone wound up betraying him. And here is Zeid bursting into laughter, exclaiming that's for sure!, that Darjis was highly respected in these parts, chieftains were at his command, he left his mark on routes and oases, his name was graven on many a rock and palm tree, sculptors of yore unwittingly carved his likeness and minted gold coins with his profile, and the desert loves him so much that, in a place known for its echoes, no matter what word you shout it is Darjis's name you hear in return (and he, too, pronounces the name with a strong accent on the second syllable). Samuel, the son of old poets from the Lebanese mountains, thinks that this is likely the most beautiful amorous ode uttered in these lands for quite some time, and looks upon Zeid with a certain admiration. But he lets nothing show.

Meanwhile, Zeid continues his soliloquy, maintaining that, of course everyone betrayed Darjis, because no one wanted to follow him. "Follow him? What for?" asks Samuel, who senses that this time he has broken the wild horse, and Zeid declares, to become king of the Arabs! And he begins, mysteriously, to laugh, then pulls the infamous ancient coin from his pocket and says that Darjis wouldn't even have needed to mint his own money, coins with his profile on them already existed, and Samuel wonders if Zeid is making fun of him, doing his little act, or if he's so in love with the Frenchman that he's lost his head and now takes him for one of those Hellenized kings of Arabia with magical names, Aretas, Rabbel, or Malichus, graven in profile on drachmas.

"So why didn't he become king?" Samuel asks.

"He wished to unite all the tribes beneath a single banner," Zeid answers. "He was mad."

"And was it because he was mad that he had me believe he couldn't speak Arabic?" Samuel asks.

"No, it was because he was a spy," Zeid replies, imperturbably.

Samuel is afraid that after a distracted answer like this the boy will take off and vanish in the dust. But Zeid keeps riding calmly by his side.

"He came among us to find out how loyal we were to the Turks and if we had ties to the British. Perhaps he was to buy us for France. In the end, he gave all that up; he had other dreams. The dreams of a madman. He truly loved the desert tribes. But the splendors of the ancient world diverted him from reality and the present."

Samuel glances curiously at the young Bedouin, who at this moment seems both serious and merry, and he realizes that, for the second time, Zeid is sending him a message. That night, in front of a thorny thicket whose shadow points backward like a sword, Samuel tells him that he is willing to pay him gold pieces, and even give him his own camel—the russet cow, nimble of step, that leads with its head and is restful for its rider, is a fabulous racer, a gift from Prince Faisal—if Zeid agrees to tell him what he knows or take him to the place where d'Argès's treasure can be found.

Zeid says nothing, but it is as if things were now settled between him and Samuel. However, the next day he starts up again with his seductive maneuvers, his sprinting and his jokes, and his restlessness seems such that Hamid declares he is not at all reassured to have that madman as a guide. In the afternoon, riders appear on the horizon and provide the two groups a cheery escort to Sheikh Raeed Hussein's camp, where they are greeted with stampeding, shots fired in the air, and dancing of all sorts. That night, in the welcome tent, around a massive platter of rice where the heads of sheep and gazelles sit enthroned, wide-eyed and mocking, Raeed Hussein, a man of fine manners and a level gaze, who looks anything but a traitor, tells Samuel that he himself helped d'Argès hide his findings at Ras es Sohr, but after the Frenchman disappeared, he thought to turn a profit. "Anyone else would've done the same," he says in justification. Then he declares that had he known someone would come on Darjis's behalf, he wouldn't have pursued this line of thought, but that, anyway, the treasure was stolen in the meantime. And naturally, he has no idea who the thief was, no doubt prowlers, looters, or a tribe that worked with Darjis and knew his plans. "And what happened to Darjis?" asks Samuel, who without realizing it has used the Arab version of the Frenchman's name. An embarrassed silence follows his question. The guests around Samuel keep reaching out to take rice and meat between their fingers, but slow their movements, waiting for their chieftain's reply. "Everyone will have told you it was I who sold him to the Turks," says Raeed. "That is a lie. He was arrested in the tent of Fayed Ibn Alaeddine, to whom he had gone to propose an alliance between the Bani Harf and the Talleat. Darjis had some mad ideas. He wished to rebuild kingdoms that never were, or existed only long ago."

Later, toward midnight, Samuel meets with Zeid on a small hillock west of camp. Fires have been lit, around which guards are seated cross-legged, rifles on their knees. Camels grunt and snore, dogs roam about, still warring over the remains of the feast. Samuel finds Zeid behind a few arbutus trees. When he appears, two figures slip furtively away, leaving the chieftain's son to his affairs. Samuel pulls his coat close over his chest; the cold is harsh. On the horizon, dozens of mountainous peaks seem a fine bluish lace which, with the vast bejeweled finery of the heavens, make a grand ball gown of the nighttime desert. At least that is what Samuel thinks as he sits down beside Zeid. "I got your father's version," he says after a long moment of silence. "But don't forget that I've promised you gifts if you tell me what you know as well." Sitting cross-legged, Zeid wraps himself in the furs that form a rug around him. "I don't want gifts," he replies. "I took Darjis's treasure from Ras es Sohr simply because I didn't want my father to sell it, especially not to the Turks." He is silent for a moment. A bit bewildered, Samuel says nothing. "My father did not sell Darjis to the Turks," Zeid continues, as if setting things straight. "But he would have sold them the treasure. In his eyes, they were not the same thing. But in mine, they were."

The next day, Samuel and his troupe leave Raeed Hussein's camp accompanied by Zeid and three of his friends, bodyguards or companions. All day long, they travel through the same strange and elephantine extravaganza, the same scattered flock of rocky ochre massifs. At night, after a rest from the heat, they reach the Mou'in well, dry this time of year, encircled by trees that are also dry, and ringed by mountains with wrinkled flanks the setting sun dyes pink and ruby red. "We are here," says Zeid, his voice tinged with nostalgia. All it takes Samuel's men is a bit of scraping at the ground by the foot of one mountain, and there they are, lying flat and only thinly buried in the sand, as if beneath summer sheets: a dozen marble and limestone bodies in a row, gods and goddesses serene and faraway of face, with full-lipped but enigmatic smiles, high cheekbones, hair pulled back, porous to eternity and at the same time locked in immemorial parley with themselves, arms stiff along torsos sometimes nude and sometimes, with the goddesses, swathed in transparent veils. Standing wordlessly beside Zeid, a dreamy Samuel has the impression this series of prostrate sculptures is like the echo of himself twelve times over, the resonance of his corporeal presence in the world. All around him, warriors and caravaners comment with uncustomary quiet on the mysterious unveiling of these stone beings. After a long moment of strange and general communion, Samuel asks Zeid if he wishes to split the treasure. Zeid replies that it all belongs to Darjis. Samuel reminds him that d'Argès no longer has anything to do with this, but Zeid shrugs. "You and Darjis are the same," he says. Then, as if to forget his sorrow, he launches himself after one of his companions, racing off barefoot, cords of silk and gold swinging from his head. The two boys roll around in the sand, laughing and wrestling to the shouts of their friends and Hamid's men and Mawlud's. In the meantime, the imperial toga of the mountains all around has darkened, growing purple, then dark lilac, and finally night falls completely; fires are lit while, off to one side, the gods and goddesses stare with their petrified eyes at the great nocturnal parade of the heavens.

10

A WEEK LATER, SAMUEL FINALLY REACHES BIR SUHEILA
and Askar Chalabi el Suheili's camp. He finds his palace intact in its thousand pieces, an open-air warehouse
spread under the sun. Beside Chalabi's tents, it seems a
cumbersome object confided to a foreigner who keeps it
grudgingly for you. Samuel takes a tour to inspect the
bronze-framed mirrors tossed facedown on the ground,
the woodwork some of whose motifs have long since vanished, been gouged out, turned into stumps or splinters,
fragments of frescoed wall where birds drinking from
basins have faded in the sun of so many deserts, coni-
cal chimneys toppled on their sides or backs like beetles,
and hundreds of scattered chunks, a good portion of
which doubtless no longer match up. Chalabi el Suheili
tells him a whole host of plausible but probably made-up
stories about the lodestone this colossal hodgepodge was
for nearby tribes, drawing Shammar and Sherrari looters, and the valiant guard his own people mounted to
protect it, and Samuel pays him off, reminding him his
words are useless and what gold has been promised will
be delivered, period, end of story.

After which they feast around platters of rice. Samuel stays with Chalabi for three days to rest before loading up his palace and his mysterious deities and setting out once more, heading north, vowing this time not to stop before reaching Lebanon. He has left his russet camel to Zeid Ibn Raeed as a souvenir, and now rides a less supple mount whose somewhat stiff steps reverberate through his body. But he is happy. Dressed in his worn-out European suit, his rebellious lock poking out from the fabric wrapped around his head, he looks like a plundering prince coming back from a raid, a conquistador returning laden with riches from a lost city. The caravan stretches out and dawdles across a desert edged with chiseled mountains. The lack of the machine gun's protection is felt, but ten of Chalabi el Suheili's warriors have jointed the escort. Every night, Samuel checks in with their chieftain, as well as with Hamid and Mawlud, and all agree it will take a fortnight to reach Damascus, if all goes well. And at first, everything does, more or less. They travel amidst lands upheaved by ancient geological cataclysms, carved by erosion, sculpted by the slow work of millennia. At times they climb, and at others, descend; then rocky valleys or the broad beds of dry torrents open, littered with flint and volcanic rock that bloody the animals' feet. But they push on, the maps Samuel spreads on the rough ground when they stop from the heat are vague, but he is content to trace, through unmistakable signs, the northward advance of the long procession transporting his real estate and part of an age-old Arabian pantheon.

After ten days, they enter the territory of the famous chieftain Unayzah Ibn Ayyad, in the area around Boutha, an oasis where a few farmers grow vegetables and tubers among the palms. In the distance, regal crests tower over Unayzah's vast camp. He himself, however, is a small man whose smooth cheeks have been cratered like the desert by smallpox. His embroidered robes and the handsome gold and silver dagger at his belt prove that he is rich and powerful. Moreover, a joyous wind flutters his tents, lifting brocaded fabrics from all sides, while the women, whose jewelry and tattoos have made them resemble illuminated manuscripts, flock to see the new arrivals. Unayzah gathers his guests in his welcome tent and for three days they gossip, drink coffee, and eat from massive platters of rice ringed by meat and crowned with oryx heads. They discuss Faisal, of course, the war, and genealogies. Unayzah calmly traces his family tree back to the Prophet's closest friends, out of pride and as if to urge his guest to do the same, without which his patronymic would appear to be forgery and imposture in flagrante delicto, for the old chieftain finds it highly incomprehensible that a Christian should bear the name of his own prestigious tribe. In answer, Samuel connects his family to ancient Arab Christian tribes allied with the Ghassanids, who left Arabia before Islam, heading first for Hauran and then the mountains of Lebanon. Next he speaks of ancestors who fought beside the Emperor of Byzantium against the Muslim armies. This last point bothers his audience a bit, which makes Samuel laugh because he had predicted as much. But Unayzah, who knows the duties of hospitality, begins to tell stories of wars and raids he led long ago with Hamid Ibn Mansour, and this eases the atmosphere. After which these descendants of glorious captains whom it amuses them to think were somehow cousins head out to hunt gazelles and ostriches, and laze over picnics amidst small vegetable gardens in the oasis of Boutha, with their rifles propped against tree trunks and the water murmuring down the channels.

A few days later, Samuel leaves again. But he does not leave alone. The entire Unayzah camp leaves with him, because it is the season of the livestock markets in Ma'an. At this time, Hamid Ibn Mansour and his people decide to return to their lands at last. The Bani Suheila press on, and for a week, Samuel's caravan marches on surrounded by the Bani Ayyad tribe, with its opulent and pompous palanquins, its brightly colored camels adorned with saddle rugs and harnesses with tassels and pompoms. These beasts of burden, laden with tents and baggage, mingle with Samuel's, carrying his moving palace and his stone gods, and all this is quite diverting to the eye, for the desert is growing ever flatter, its peaks rounder, subsiding and disappearing. For three days, they travel together. Then the Bani Ayyad go on their way toward

Ma'an where Samuel does not wish to go. The city is a center for the Ottoman army, and he is not yet ready to look a Turkish officer in the eye, not to mention that his unusual cargo might arouse quite a few questions. And so Unayza Ibn Ayyad pitches his ceremonial tent amidst rocky hills the women drape with their washing, ablaze with color as their skin is with tattoos and their bodies are with ruby and vermilion robes. During one last banquet, the old chieftain gives Samuel some advice for the rest of his journey. Then he offers him fifteen warriors as an escort, led by his son Kays, to whom he declares before all assembled that he must go wherever our cousin *Samouyil* goes, and if it happens to be all the way to Damascus, then so be it, my son, you shall go all the way to Damascus.

But Kays will not go all the way to Damascus. After a few days' travel, first through slightly mountainous hills, then once more through the oft-crossed rocky beds of dry wadis, great breaches broad as valleys, which the caravan must descend into, then climb back out of each time, Fahim el Mawlud begins to grow restive, complaining about how long the journey is taking, balking before each and every effort until one morning, south of Iasa, he decrees that he will go no farther. Samuel takes him to one side and mentions gold, but Mawlud says that has nothing to do with it; the voyage is too long, he repeats, and it will never end. Samuel doesn't believe a word of this, for coming from a caravaner who up till now has been richly compensated, these are not credible excuses. Finally, Mawlud confesses his real reasons. The farther north they go, the closer they get to more heavily patrolled regions where the Turks are more greatly to be feared, and he is afraid that, as they commandeer all beasts of burden for their army, they will come and confiscate his camels and those of his clan. Samuel says nothing, but an hour later, gathers his escort, announces that he wishes to press on, and warns them that he is not about to let himself be abandoned in the middle of the desert, indicating that his warriors will not be kind to mutineers or deserters. Naturally, Mawlud spends the next few days sulking, and Samuel reflects that he could quite simply commandeer the animals himself, and sideline the man, or else sidestep the camel drivers, which would not be very hard, so generously is he paying them. But Mawlud has also been their employer for a long time, and there is nothing to imply that they will dissociate themselves from him so easily. As for his own Bedouins, they are from two different tribes, which is never a good thing, and moreover the Bani Suheila are ever less dependable; they, too, seem to be starting to feel too far from their lands. Suddenly Samuel feels weary, but one morning he finds a solution.

*

It is, at first, nothing but a train at a standstill in the middle of the desert, a short black snake come to a halt, surprised by who knows what in the dust and white light, halfway between the stations of Hasa and Qatraneh. Through his binoculars, Samuel studies the passengers, who have stepped out in the shade of the cars; the locomotive has apparently broken down and the two stokers are perched atop it. It is but a small train, two passenger cars and three or four of goods which, with Kays and three warriors, Samuel slowly approaches. When the passengers see five armed Bedouins ride up, faces shrouded, they gather at the foot of the train while the stokers on the boiler straighten up and watch. Upon reaching the train, Samuel realizes the passengers are almost all soldiers—officers, but not Turks, rather Germans and Austrians with a few wives, ladies in hats leaning out the windows, one of whom, moved by curiosity but not wishing to expose her face to the searing air, opens her parasol outside the car. Meanwhile, to avoid any misunderstanding that might end badly, especially as the officers have begun reaching for their sidearms, and rifles instead of umbrellas are poking out the through the windows of the second car, Samuel has unwound the cloth of his keffiyeh and is now advancing with his face unhidden, greeting them in Arabic and asking, with an amused air, if anyone speaks the language. Then he follows up in French, asking the same question. Officers and civilians alike are no doubt astounded by his light-skinned face, albeit darkened by a severe tan, his Anglo-Saxon mustache, and above all the fact that he is speaking French. Samuel's European slacks and his boots dangling from his saddle round out the confusion. One officer answers aggressively that they speak German here, or Turkish at the outside, but before Samuel can react, and no doubt fearing an unexpected reaction on his part, another younger officer declares with the barest trace of an accent that in fact everyone speaks and understands French. Samuel then inquires what the matter is. The officer explains, pointing at the boiler (a Jung or rather a Hartman 1910, Samuel thinks, remembering what he learned in Al-Wajh about the Turkish rail forces and the little German locomotives, even as his gaze slips slowly along the steam engine, from the cylinders down the coupling rods, stopping at the spigot on the water tank), that they have had a breakdown, and now here they are waiting for repairs, or for the station at Qatraneh to send out a patrol to investigate the delay. The officer has no doubt added this last part to put Samuel's odd-looking group off any possible mischief. Samuel is about to ask if he can help in any way, to demonstrate his peaceful intent, when behind him, in an inadvertent dramatic reversal, as if he'd just summoned them with some imperceptible sign, another group of Bani Ayyad warriors appear, followed by Bani Suheila warriors and behind them, the first groups of packsaddle camels with their cargo. What seemed at first to the officers and the train's passengers a small number of pillagers now looks like an entire tribe. Before their eyes, Samuel transforms into a kind of adventurer leading plunder-hungry nomads to war, who have picked as their target a train broken down in the middle of the vast stony void of the desert, with neither machine guns nor armor plating, its passengers surprised while lounging about or stupidly stretching their legs. There are indeed rifles poking out the windows of the second car, but they won't be enough against what, to the German and Austrian soldiers still reeling from surprise, now seems like an army of Bedouins. To put them at ease, Samuel suggests the officers tell their soldiers to lower their weapons. Meanwhile, his own warriors have lined up beside him, and he curbs their tendency to want to surround the train, recommending their rifles remain pointed at the sky. At the moment, one of the soldiers, also speaking French, but with a strong accent and a firm but not yet bellicose tone, asks Samuel just what it is he wants. And so, with a mocking smile, his gaze dancing an imperceptible saraband, Samuel offers to send his men to the stations in Hasa and Qatraneh to notify them of the locomotive's breakdown, but on one condition. The officers and the handful of civilians are silent for a moment, baffled, waiting for the next part, which gives Samuel the chance to examine them and deduce that they are all Austrians, no doubt returning from Ma'an, or even Medina. And since he has not said a word, one of the Austrians, with great sideburns, asks what his condition is, and Samuel declares that actually, well, his condition is that he'd like to take a bath.

With these words, Samuel pivots his camel a quarter-turn and, passing between his warriors and the officers, he rides up to the engine and calls out to the stokers, who descend from atop the boiler. They are Syrian, Samuel speaks with them, and still atop his mount, he heads for the water tank. There, at last, he bids his mount kneel, slips off, and for a good dozen minutes, like Louis XIV among his courtiers, or any Oriental despot far-fetched of whim, he washes himself at the spigot, the water from which is quite hot. The warriors and caravaners assembled to one side laugh and make amused commentary, while the Austrians appear to be calmly awaiting the end of what they consider a worrisome ritual whose follow-up they fear. That is why they are not laughing, and are quite likely considering possible actions to take against these strange aggressors. But the Bedouins are watchful and no one makes a move except Samuel who, rid of his old military slacks, his tatty tunic, and his Arab headgear, is scrubbing himself with pumice collected from the oasis in Boutha. Then he lets himself dry off as he rummages about in his saddlebags. After which he dons another pair of slacks and a dress shirt and pulls on his boots, which he has also rinsed off. Once all this is done, he walks over to the group of soldiers who at this point no doubt take him for a madman, a plundering chieftain who finds amusement in staging lugubrious scenes before slaughtering his enemies. He stops before what looks to him like the highest ranking officer, to judge by the insignia and the number of stars on his uniform, the one who spoke first, likely a colonel, who is now standing with his arms crossed in a stance of impotent defiance—and Samuel introduces himself. He says that he is a Lebanese merchant, with a caravan of merchandise he has been transporting for years through desert and savannah, which explains why the presence of running water, even from a locomotive cistern, exerts an irresistible appeal on him. The officers and civilians have drawn cautiously closer and are listening to this strange character who has, in yet a third metamorphosis, become a perfectly civil merchant, with what seem to them impeccable French and manners. They've gotten over their initial surprise when Samuel summons four Bani Ayyad and, after listening to the two stokers and asking the highest-ranking officer if he has any special message to pass on to the two stations, he dispatches all four riders with word that train number 118 has broken down at Kilometer 402, a problem with the flue in the smokebox.

*

Meanwhile, at the foot of a small stony hill, Kays has pitched a tent where Samuel invites the passengers to take their rest. After exchanging glances, trading imperceptible queries with eyes and lips, the officers make for the tent, their pleasure—concealed, or laced with apprehension—all the greater since the wagons have by now become veritable ovens. Samuel says the women, too, are welcome to join them in the shade, and so pleasant is his declaration that the three ladies are sent for while, for their part, the Turkish soldiers have ventured from the second car and, despite everything, remain on their guard. Inside the tent, the Bedouins have readied coffee; the coffeepots with their graceful curves mingle with the folded parasols, the silken cords from Kays's keffiyeh with the ladies' veils, the Arab chieftain's caftans with the dresses, epaulettes, and braids on chests. Samuel is sorry no Orientalist painter is on hand to capture this incredible scene, but he is proud to have composed it himself. He has also kissed the hands of the three women—one of whom he finds quite pretty—so perfectly when they entered the tent that the atmosphere has suddenly relaxed. Pleasantries and general information are exchanged. Samuel explains that he is heading for Damascus and hopes to reach Beirut; his guests say that they are on their way from Medina, that they are a logistical support battalion, and their little train was specially chartered for them in Ma'an. And so they chatter on until the officers ask Samuel about his cargo, whereupon he invites everyone on a small guided tour of his Arab palace and his museum of deities. The mirrors, the ornate wooden ceilings, and the silent gods are all unswaddled as if before prestigious bidders at an auction. The Austrians stop taking Samuel for a madman or an eccentric, and now see him as a kind of Sinbad or

Marco Polo of the deserts, with his goods from another era. Somberly, the officers brush the frescoed panels with their fingers, as if experts; the women look the gods in the eye then turn away, overwhelmed by their expressions; one of the officers, upon discovering the Roman helmet, observes that German armies still use crests, and Samuel is unable to tell if this is irony or a sign of pride. After which all return to the refuge of the tent, for the soles of their feet are beginning to burn, and there, as they sip the coffee that makes the rounds of those gathered in two small glasses passed from hand to hand, they trade tales of houses put up, taken down, or lugged about over hill and dale. Samuel tells the story of that man who had himself a mansion built on the outskirts of Beirut in the posh style of residences in town, but when it was done, he found it not to his liking, because among other things it wasn't facing the way he wanted, so he had it demolished and rebuilt with the façade oriented as desired. Kays, whose sumptuous attire of watered silk and brocaded keffiyeh brings out his dark eyes, keeps catching the women's glances, and speaking next, he tells more for their sake than anyone else's an anecdote he heard one day from a Syrian merchant, while Samuel translates. It is the story of a Druze prince who fell in love with a rococo marble parlor in a Damascus villa, bought it, had it dismantled and transported to his home in the mountains of Lebanon, where he ordered that an entire palace be built to serve as its setting. When he is done, it is one of the Austrian officers' turn to tell the story of a Salzburg aristocrat who fell in love not with a palace but the echo that arose from a footfall on the terrace of a mansion outside Florence, and so it was that the man bought the mansion, had it carefully dismantled and moved to his home near Salzburg, where he had it rebuilt. But the officer continues in almost unaccented French, which Samuel translates for Kays and the other Arabs, to the aristocrat's utter amazement, the terrace no longer produced the same musical echo that was more beautiful to his ears than a Mozart opera. And so he had the scenery around his home redone to match the environs of Florence; he had soil brought in from Tuscany, Tuscan pines, Tuscan pebbles—but, the officer concludes, it was no good, the echo had remained in Italy.

Toward evening, fires are lit and a meal prepared, and that is when a track inspection car announces itself with a whistle from the south. It brings engineers from Hasa with spare parts for the locomotive. This does not stop the Arabs and the Austrians from feasting. Then the Austrians discreetly invite Samuel to pop over for a drink in their car, if the liqueurs have managed to withstand the heat. And withstand it they have; toasts are made and cigars savored while from outside rings the sound of iron and workers hammering on the locomotive by firelight. "These caravans on rails are inferior to the good old caravans on legs," one of the officers proclaims, which makes everyone laugh. They drink to the health of caravans on legs soon to go the way of the dodo, after which, and before retiring, Samuel asks, like a schoolboy at the end of summer camp, if the members of this merry company will each jot him a little something on some old sheet of paper to remember them by, since he can't commemorate them all with a photo. The women find the idea charming, the men deem it a bit too romantic, but since all are excessively merry from drink, they play along. On a large sheet of paper with the letterhead of the Fourth Turkish Army, each of them writes a little comment, laughing all the while, about showers in the desert and moving palaces, followed by a handsome signature. In the enthusiasm born of too many glasses of liqueur, some add their names and addresses in Damascus, even Vienna; the pretty young woman adds her address in Salzburg like a mischievous wink beside the address in Damascus her husband has written with slightly wobbly downstrokes, and the next morning Samuel parades this piece of paper about when they strike camp. He shows it to Mawlud, to the caravaners, to the Bani Suheila and their chieftain, declaring that this is a letter of safe passage; with it, they can go anywhere they want. Naturally he feels remorse at telling tales and deceiving his men, but at the same time reflects that, after all, these handsome-sounding names of ranking officers and imposing signatures might absolutely impress a Turkish patrol tempted by the idea of commandeering their camels. But they do not run into any such patrols, and for four days, this little ploy helps everyone push on without fear. Mawlud remains quiet, as do his companions, and they finish skirting Palestine, where the frontlines of the war have moved; they head up deserts with stony hills, then across broad lands with scattered crops around Daraa, until they reach the heart of the Hauran, sixty miles south of Damascus.

11

IT IS COMMON KNOWLEDGE THAT DURING THE FIRST
World War, almost all Arab officers in Ottoman armies
were more or less won over to Prince Faisal's cause,
with the result that many were confined to routine and
minor postings far from the front. As the war went on, a
number of them, Syrians and Mesopotamians, took the
plunge and deserted in order to join up with the Hashemite forces. But some never had the chance, or kept
wavering till the end, or waited in vain for an occasion
that never presented itself. This must have been the case
with the officer who commanded the small fortress of
Khirbat al-Harik, north of Daraa in the Hauran, on the
route Samuel Ayyad was taking in his journey toward
Lebanon. To call Khirbat al-Harik a fortress is, moreover,
an exaggeration; it had doubtless been a large farm long
ago, built amidst cultivated fields on the ruins of some
edifice erected in the time of Emperor Philip the Arab,
like the temples in Al-Sanamayn and the nearby town of
Bosra. And so it is that in early autumn 1917, as Samuel
Ayyad draws near, the officer in charge of this fortress is
calmly awaiting Faisal's armies, a bit as others awaited

the Tartars, though he does so in hopes of joining them. And to while away the time, he maintains law and order in his district, where, in truth, not much happens. The local peasants are a quiet sort, seeing to their fruit trees, growing their watermelons, and harvesting their wheat without fuss, such that Colonel Ghaleb Jabri has nothing to do. The lands around him run flat to infinity, and are on all sides bounded by the desert, from which he hopes one day to see the Arab armies emerge. And so, this descendant of an old aristocratic Damascene family often goes hunting and receives chieftains from neighboring villages, with whom he discusses the war, harvests, and military requisitioning over endless games of chess or checkers. He also receives, but in secret, certain swaggering *abadays* from Jabal al-Druze, braggart outlaws wanted by Ottoman justice for their actions against the Sultan's army, such as the infamous Talal Harethedin, with whom he has a good time laughing at anecdotes about life among the mountain folk, or listening to updates more credible than those of official reports on the state of the war and its fronts, afterward showing his visitor out an ancient, condemned door that he has secretly restored to working order. And then, when there are no hunts, or town worthies or abadays to receive, nor mail from Daraa or Damascus to read, Ghaleb Jabri himself leads routine patrols along the paths between the villages, and in the desert to the south. And it is while leading such a patrol one morning that he comes upon

Samuel Ayyad's endless caravan, endless because in his eyes, so many camels trotting so nonchalantly along can only be an illusion—or else these are the armies of Faisal. But of course, Ghaleb Jabri knows that it is neither one nor the other, and with his patrol of ten horsemen, he rides to the front of this singular apparition.

Samuel, for his part, has spotted him. For three days, he has been advancing according to his men's intuitions and his own, or else the often vague directions of shepherds they run across in the hollows of the wadis. When he sees the Turkish patrol approaching, he waves at his companions to settle down, and here, already, is Ghaleb Jabri. He is a man serene of face, almost blond, with a mole just above his light-colored mustache. More from the color of his skin than his uniform and his *kalpak*, Samuel takes him for a Turk, but the officer speaks first, in the beautiful Arabic of the Damascus area. He demands an explanation for what he sees; Samuel replies in Arabic that is no less beautiful, and between Jabri and Samuel, it is hard to tell who is more surprised. Nevertheless, Samuel explains his presence here, telling the same story: that he is a merchant transporting goods from far-flung corners of the desert, and he hopes to reach Damascus with his cargo, then Beirut. Meanwhile, the caravan has slowly bunched up; they are in the middle of lands that bear traces of very ancient plowing. Kays and the other chieftains form a handsome guard around Samuel. Behind them, the warriors stand like a long hedge encroaching on the fields and the old, hardened furrows. Their rifles are out in plain sight, and the ends of their line edge forward imperceptibly, and slowly they surround the Turks. But Jabri cares not a whit, he asks Samuel how he plans on reaching Damascus, and Samuel replies that he thinks he will continue north, that in truth he has no maps and is feeling his way along a bit blindly. Jabri remains silent for a moment. Samuel senses trouble, and seeks an alternative—the Austrian autographs, perhaps, but he knows that will never work with a colonel—and it takes him a moment to realize the officer has started speaking again, and what he is saying is that he has maps back at the fort, and they can consult them there. Then he adds that he will also, of course, proceed to check on the contents of what the animals are carrying.

*

In these early autumn days, the sky is vast, cleansed of summer's whiteness, the earth exults, and the long line of camels, with its horseback Turkish escort, makes it way among orchards of plum and apricot trees that shine like mirrors, along low walls bordering these gardens at the desert's edge. Then come more fields where the wheat has been mown and gathered, and finally the fortress of Khirbat appears. While the soldiers rummage idly through the caravan's load in the courtyard and in front of the main gates, Samuel is Jabri's guest. He has taken off his keffiyeh, slipped on his boots, and is sitting in a wicker armchair in the colonel's company on a terrace of the singular fortress-farm, and the two men are talking about the war. Jabri tells of how the Arabs led by Lawrence and Sherif Nasir took Aqaba. Then he brings over a military map which he unfolds between himself and Samuel, who soon realizes Jabri needs some entertainment. Moreover, the colonel offers to let Samuel sleep in the fortress instead of camping out with the Arabs. The proposition surprises Samuel, but Jabri's gaze is honest and generous, if admittedly a bit languid, like his entire bearing, which demonstrates in all things a cordial, disinterested, and uninsistent friendliness; one feels obliged to accept his offers, made though they are as if from a distance and an understated word or a wave of the hand with which the colonel seems to leave the choice entirely up to his guest. But when Samuel agrees to stay, Jabri seems happy, has a dinner of meat, vegetables, and fruit served that delights Samuel, who hasn't tasted any fruit but dates for months. That entire evening, as they eat, then each smoke a cigar, settled in comfortable armchairs, and even as they stroll about the terraces of the fortified farm, the soldier and the adventurer chat away, their conversation wholly based upon a deliberately maintained case of mistaken identity. Jabri, who has discreetly studied Samuel's military attire, is soon convinced he is dealing not only with a Lebanese merchant but perhaps one of the Arab officers in the British Army serving Faisal. But he makes no allusion to this. As for Samuel, he has indeed noticed how little enthusiasm the colonel has for his duties and his barely disguised jubilation while recounting the conquest of Aqaba. And so, for him, Jabri's sympathy for the Arab Revolt is undeniable. But he says nothing either, and for part of the night, the two men build their exchange around the politely unspoken, which spares them mutual embarrassment even as it allows them to speak freely. They discuss the towns where they were born, the situation in Syria, and also, inevitably, the remainder of Samuel's voyage, the route he has picked. Jabri advises him to avoid Damascus and head west, toward Mount Hermon, and to cross it at its lowest point, emerging into the Bekaa not far from the town of Rashaya. Samuel finds this a capital idea, but brings up commandeering and his companions' reluctance. Jabri tells him they are right, so many animals traveling under armed Arab escort is an unusual sight in the region right now; he himself can cover their journey up till the edges of his district, but after that it will be harder, and at any rate, the best thing to do would be to travel by night. After some quick calculations, Jabri concludes that three nights will be enough to reach Mount Hermon.

Though Samuel is perfectly satisfied with this arrangement, his caravaners and the Bani Suheila, on the other hand, will hear none of it. When Samuel explains his plans for the nights to come, it is mutiny all over again.

If a letter of safe passage from the Austrian Army and the friendship of a Turkish colonel are not enough to guarantee safe passage by day, Mawlud observes, then it is proof that the journey is considerably dangerous. Samuel has no rejoinder to this: he calls on their courage, solidarity, the lure of gold—but all in vain. Mawlud orders his people to prepare to turn back south, and they obey, for they are starting to fear for their lives. The Bani Suheila reach the same decision. At noon, over another meal in the warm autumn light, the colonel advises Samuel to let his people go, and promises to look into finding a replacement for the caravan himself. Samuel pictures his massive cargo on mules or Ottoman army wagons, and the idea doesn't please him much, but Jabri, who notices the sudden distance in his guest's eyes, reassures him.

"There are many pack animals in the region," he says. "They remain unseen because they are well hidden."

"And you're going to commandeer them for me?" Samuel asks laughingly.

"I could," Jabri says, amused, giving in for a moment to the mannered protraction of his Damascus accent. "But the people around here are friends. If you have the wherewithal to pay them generously, they may agree to come out with their creatures and undertake the risk. They know the land. They will not fear traveling by night."

*

First thing the next day, after Mawlud and the Bani Suheila have left for their deserts, and only Kays and his men remain, Samuel and Jabri set out on horseback for an exploratory tour of the surrounding villages. They cross through fields toward farms, or head down roads from one village to the next. They are welcomed into bare interiors, sit cross-legged on mats, and Jabri outlines the request to each owner of a packhorse or mule. Then Samuel makes his offer, and eyes widen in astonishment. When a deal has been struck, all drink coffee or blackberry syrup, after which Samuel pays the villagers an advance, and they look puzzled and embarrassed, for what the Lebanese hands out under the consenting gaze of the Ottoman officer are British gold pieces. "Aren't you afraid of traitors and informers, Ghaleb bey?" Samuel asks as they leave the house of an old peasant who seems ambivalent. Jabri shrugs. "There's no one an informer can squeal to about but me," he replies, laughing. From this moment on, each accomplice understands that the other can read him like an open book, and the chivalrous ceremony with which they have been treating each other becomes pointless. This nonetheless gives way to heated discussions, notably at noon, during a lunch where Samuel and Colonel Jabri work systematically from the basic premise that the Ottoman empire will soon be defeated. Arab independence is thus their favorite subject, but they have doubts and fears. Jabri says the Lebanese Christians desire an independent state and will refuse to hear out Faisal. Samuel retorts by demanding if the people of Damascus, who so fiercely want an independent Arab state, will manage to hear out the prince's unruly Bedouins. Jabri sighs, the mole above his mustache, which the star and crescent on his shirt collar quite stylishly echo, shivers for a moment. He looks out at the horizon, where he no doubt expects to see those famous Bedouins arriving at last, not suspecting that in under three months he will have abandoned his post and joined up with Lawrence and Sherif Ali in Azraq, one hundred and twenty miles south of Khirbat al-Harik. A long silence sets in, a silence that is like a gift of the desert the desert spreads over the orchards of plum and apricot trees, the fields of melons and watermelons, a silence that only the *click-clack* of waterwheels on the canal that crosses the fields has marked with its placid, endless cadence for centuries, for millennia, from the time of the Byzantine empire, the kingdom of the Nabataeans, and the biblical prophets. Then a corporal comes offering coffee, Jabri takes out his cigars, and lights his own, declaring that only the Almighty knows the future, and they shall see.

After a week, about forty mules and just as many horses have been rounded up by venturing fairly far afield into remote hamlets in the Hauran. These aren't enough, but by overburdening the beasts and going slowly, it should work. The night before they are to assemble, after an evening spent in the company of two town worthies, Colonel Ghaleb Jabri receives Talal Harethedin, the hero of Jabal al-Druze, with his great mustache and his bandolier of cartridges across his chest. Talal arrives in the dark of the night, curious about the troupe soon to leave for Rashaya. For a few long minutes, he looks Samuel up and down with an eagle eye, listening to him speak, sitting in an armchair and smoothing his mustache. Then, once his examination seems to have convinced him, he offers to act as a guide and bring along a few friends as an escort. Three days later, Samuel Ayyad's new caravan is gathered in the fortified farm. They load up the palace and the unconcerned deities on a moonless night. The courtyard is noisy and labored, the gods are hauled from the shed and dumped amidst the dust and the dung, waiting to be hitched up; the great mirrors are leaned against fissured walls like planks from some old sideboard; and the elaborate windows, the fragments of roof and frescoed wall, lie scattered in all directions. Samuel tries to bring some order to the proceedings, gets angry, and then gives up. While the Bani Ayyad look on amused, squatting around the courtyard and not lifting a finger, everything is hoisted up on horseback or mule-back and, around midnight, the convoy rattles off. An hour later, beneath a pair of hackberry trees, they find Talal's Druze waiting as promised. When the drivers recognize the hero and his friends, all famous in the region, they give free rein to their joy and relief. A long rustle of laughter, joking, and muffled shouts travels up the convoy. It must be said that the martial air of the new arrivals, their curving mustaches, *sirwals*, and bodies bristling with weapons are a heartening sight. Talal goes over to Samuel now, speaking loudly, laughing, and making quite the din, but this is more reassuring to the troupe than a banner or a brightly colored pennant. His companions also speak noisily while the Bani Ayyad, silently perched on their camels, remain distant and brooding.

*

For four nights they advance beneath the vast opulence of a sky that seems so close they could reach out and touch its cold, teeming light with their hands. The mule-drivers and the peasants move merrily along, feeling rich perhaps with the wealth of the great black cloak covering them above but especially the coins in the pockets of their robes and sirwals which make them call out to one another in the dark, conferring or humming quietly as they walk. They head northwest, avoiding villages and inhabited farms. And since the rules are now reversed, as soon as day breaks they stop, so as not to risk running afoul of farmers in their fields, shepherds, or mere travelers. Once they stop at a farm that has been abandoned because of the war, draft, and famine, another time in a fallow orchard amidst lands last plowed three or four seasons ago, no doubt for similar reasons. In the courtyard, or under trees whose wrinkled fruit makes for only a meager harvest, the men lie down to sleep. Those who do not sleep unwrap their victuals; Talal's companions and the Bani Ayyad make frugal meals, then groups form around the Druze abadays who recount their exploits for the company's laughter and entertainment. As these strapping lads are a prideful sort, they speak only when asked, even waiting to be coaxed and cajoled a bit, then launch into their oft-told tales of policemen they've bamboozled, too-rich dignitaries they've dumped naked by the side of the road, and trains intercepted in open country. One day, it is Samuel who tells how in Beirut, the most fearsome abadays had a habit of gathering at a café on Place des Canons, where they played dominos and smoked hookah pipes, and there anyone with a matter of honor to settle or a wrong to right would come to find them, until one morning the café roof collapsed because a wooden column had given way. And yet continues Samuel, all the abadays escaped unharmed for the very good reason that there was no one in the café that morning, as one and all were at the funeral of Elias Halabi, the most famous among them, who had died the night before and in so doing, saved the lives of all his fellows. Everyone applauds, laughs, marvels at the power of chance or the will of the Almighty, after which, little by little, sleep sets in. If they are on a farm and its surrounding fields, they each seek a place in the empty but shady rooms, then flee the swelter in these rooms when they fill up. If they are in an orchard, they hasten to the cool shade, also a favorite of flies. Then, in late afternoon, they play checkers or dominos, groom and curry the animals, ready themselves, loading up pieces of the palace and the statues of gods. Day wanes bit by bit, the clouds like rocky metaphors of Al-Hejaz grow tinged with violet, then pink, then gray; night falls, and they resume their travels, in the already brisk chill.

*

But staying hidden has its disadvantages. The second night is very dark, the sky cloudy, it seems perfect until suddenly a flare-up of ever more furious barking reveals they've come too close to a village that has remained invisible in the tarry darkness. The middle and tail end of the columns react well, spread out but stay in touch. The mules with the bronze-framed mirrors and the horses with the woodwork mashrabiyas scatter in every direction, pieces of the palace and the statues of deities dispersing in the dark, while Samuel, Talal, and those in the lead fall back chaotically at the shouts and injunctions of locals, who have emerged from their houses with rifles and are blindly shooting every which way. Samuel's group does not reply in kind, but keeps retreating. Luckily, the villagers do not think to set out in pursuit, or else lack the means; they settle for gathering by the light of their oil lamps for a hunt that stops short. Two hours later, the line has re-formed in a silence full of rallying murmurs and muffled exclamations. The next night, it is the caravan's tail end that violently erupts into inexplicable agitation. In the space of a few seconds, the animals are caught up in a tremendous panic, snorting, kicking, rearing fearsomely, as if something were harrying them along from behind, and gradually the disorder takes hold of the entire troupe. From the rear, cries, mad whinnying mixed with howls indicate an incomprehensible battle between the men, their animals, and forces sprung up from the night. Samuel rushes back, along with Druze riders and Bani Ayyad, and what he glimpses at first is a flurry of shapes, whirling at the heart of a spurt of black blood. Then he sees a packhorse on its side, thrashing with a dark, spotted form that seems to cling fast to it, jolting it this way and that in a horrible choreography. It takes him another few seconds to spot the horse's owner, in an almost hysterical rage, shouting things that can't be made out and desperately whipping the attacker without daring to get any closer, as if trying to fight too fierce a flame. Finally Samuel pulls his revolver from his belt, but he can't get a clear shot because of the man with the whip, whom Talal is shouting at to step aside, and in the end it is Kays, no doubt used to fighting panthers and lions in the desert, who fires three shots from his rifle, sending the beast sprung from the shadows flying life-lessly, almost nonchalantly, off to one side.

The rest of the night is devoted to restoring peace and order to the somewhat traumatized troupe. The dead horse is abandoned and Samuel compensates its owner. The deity it was carrying hasn't suffered much, but when they unwrap it, they find it spattered with blood. As for the panther, whose presence in these parts is a mystery to all concerned: Kays carries off its regal corpse hoping to skin it during a long diurnal stopover. But there is no stopover, for in the morning they find no suitable place to rest. Still, the landscape has gradually become desertlike again, and there is hardly any risk of bad run-ins; a quick scan of the four cardinal directions is enough to convince even the most skeptical. And so, despite general exhaustion, they push on, and nonetheless, have a bad run-in. It does not come from the north, or the south, or any point on the compass. However, the drone is clearly audible; eyes scan the line where land meets sky but nothing disturbs its perfect rectilinearity, imperceptibly wavering in the heat. Then the noise becomes clearer, more mechanical, and Samuel suddenly realizes it is coming from the sky. He looks up; soon the entire caravan is looking up and everyone sees, in the middle of the sky, two Turkish planes, two strange birds with stacked wings on the approach, doubtless returning to Damascus from the base at Ma'an, hovering in the ether, buzzing and sputtering. Powerless, furious, Samuel thinks this is the worst thing that could happen, that if those planes spot the convoy, which is quite likely, and find it unusual, he can expect a large armed patrol shortly. When the two vehicles pass directly overhead, the fascinated peasants and mule-drivers cannot keep themselves from shouting and waving their hands, forgetting that it is a Turkish patrol, unable to perceive in the flying objects they are seeing for the first time anything other than an unbelievable miracle, a marvel made by other men that transcends the differences between them. But soon they realize their mistake. For the planes, after seeming to go on their way for a bit, wheel around and return, like curious creatures sniffing out something suspect with their muzzles, and now here they are again, dipping a wing so the pilots can get a better look at what's down below. They make one more turn, show themselves once more, and then fly off again, until they are soon but two distant, worrisome dots in the sky; then they vanish completely, and the desert returns to its millenarian stillness.

For the rest of the day, the caravaners advance without taking their eyes from the horizon. Far off to the south odd, bare little mountains appear, like overturned cups, relieving the severity of the other contours. Despite exhaustion and thirst, they do not stop, heading straight west, at the edge of which the sun deigns to venture at last, after what has seemed an endless and hardly amicable posting in the middle of the sky. It is in their eyes now, but what they want is to see it finally set down and vanish, which it soon does; the sun takes its leave, giving way to a layer of vivid pink that turns crimson, and then soon it is night. In the early coolness, they stop for a few hours, then head out again. Their feet are swollen and numb, their bodies totter, Samuel and the Druze riders lend their horses to the most exhausted peasants, while the mule-drivers show spectacular endurance. In the middle of the night, languorously lit by a shard of reappeared moon, ghosts of small trees begin dotting the land, the relief of the terrain grows more uneven, more abrupt in places. Just as day trembles on the verge of breaking and makes its cold felt, they finally stop by a grove of dwarf trees. When the sun—not the sun of the evening before, but another sun, a young, triumphant sun, handsome and generous—rises, preceded by Venus, the morning star, the laughing goddess with chignons of arbutus trees and holm oak, everyone realizes they are in the foothills of Mount Hermon.

12

ON ITS EASTERN FLANK, MOUNT HERMON RISES IN A gentle slope. It is a venerable mountain, sown with junipers and holm oak, species that dislike a lack of privacy and look like flocks grazing freely in lines scattered over vast spaces. Springs gush up here, there, and everywhere; snow from the summits provides small cataracts in winter, which makes Mount Hermon the boundary stone of the deserts' reign, a foretaste of Lebanon's verdant splendors. For two days, the exhausted caravan takes its rest beneath a vast and gentle autumn sky in the hollow of a small dale where a cold stream runs. After which they leave once more, and there are no deserters, everyone presses on. Talal and his companions claim they have relatives in Rashaya, and the Bani Ayyad wish no matter the cost to see Lebanon, the dream of all the Arab tribes. They make their way north, veering slowly west, climbing mountains, descending into valleys flocked by dwarf trees, then haul themselves uphill once more. After a day, the altitude gain makes itself felt in the air's coolness and clarity. Sensing that the Beqaa and Mount Lebanon are about to appear, Samuel almost involuntarily slows the pace. They make camp beneath walnut and plane trees. The cold is harsh; they make a small fire to roast a few pheasants. The next day, Samuel tells his men he has a gift for them, and an hour later, as if he had been planning it for ages, as if he had wandered desert and savannah for years on end only to experience this pleasure in his heart and eyes at last, he reaches a promontory where he sees before him, granted in one fell swoop, plush and abundant, the Beqaa Valley, that rich carpet of crops tossed at Lebanon's feet, and the nave of Lebanon itself. This stretches northward as far as the eye can see, wooded in patches with brief manes of pine, sculpted by terraced farms; from its flanks at regular intervals rise, like frail pillars joining it with the heavens, placid columns of smoke from the fires of woodcutters who for millennia have slowly consumed its cedars, cypresses, and oaks. From his vantage, Samuel can also take in at a glance, as if in succession, the series of rounded summits that make up its crown: Mount Barouk, Mount Sannine, Mount Keserwan, whose names he murmurs softly to himself before offering all this up wordlessly to his men who, one by one, emerge onto the mound where they stand and receive full force the spectacle of this promised land.

*

After half a day's rest, they begin their descent toward the Beqaa, along the west side of Mount Hermon. A few cultivated terraces appear. Lower, no doubt, lie the few hamlets these mountains hold. As for Rashaya, it is slightly off to the south. When night falls, they camp in a small clearing. Out of caution, they light no fire, but warm themselves with talk. Talal readies to leave for Rashaya tomorrow, where he claims he has a cousin who once fled the Hauran because of an obscure quarrel, and could serve as a guide the rest of the way. As for the Arabs, Samuel is wondering if the vision of Lebanon has satisfied them, when Kays announces that in the morning he will turn back, happy to have seen what he has seen but reflecting that, having come this far, from here on out he will no longer be able to return without difficulty; his weapons and his camels are too obvious, and his men too few to be able to defend themselves properly in unknown lands. That night, huddled up in his blanket and Bedouin furs, Samuel does not sleep. The night is so bright now, and the moon so present that the small trees make shadows on the diaphanous earth. Beneath heavens of nocturnal illumination, he thinks that he is at last nearing the end of his long wandering, not suspecting that it has not yet sprung upon him its last surprise, nor offered him its final encounter.

In the morning, he decides to go with Talal to Rashaya. While the scattered horses and mules are seen to and coffee makes the rounds, perfuming the air, he shaves and dresses before one of the mirrors that have reflected the faces of Roman and Sicilian princesses, sultans, and Moorish slaves. Talal laughingly asks if he is about to ask for someone's hand in marriage, and Samuel muses that this morning will be his first contact with a town from his native land, and this prompts attention over his appearance. For the first time in months and months, instead of an Arab keffiyeh with its cords, he dons a hat. Then he mounts a horse. The two men cross over hills, sometimes at a gallop, sometimes stopping to talk, then springing again on the horses, spurring them abruptly forward and driving them to outdo themselves, shouting joyously and calling out to each other as if each savoring a freedom of movement that the caravan's pace made impossible. They have been riding for over an hour and are nearing Rashaya when, at the bottom of a vale, Samuel lifts a hand and pulls up short. When Talal draws abreast, Samuel points out what he's seen—an automobile parked under the pines, with no sign of life about. The presence of such a vehicle near Rashaya surprises him; he moves forward, looking for a human being, and then he hears laughter and bright voices. They're coming from a bit higher up, on the far side beyond the vehicle. He heads over, his curiosity aroused; the laughter is light, high-pitched, flutters and falls again like a pattering rain, cool and graceful. It is the laughter of women. Talal, too, has recognized it, and follows Samuel toward it. Samuel advances among the scattered trees as if through a tiny labyrinth and comes upon them at last: four young women under a walnut tree, not in the still-cool shade but right out in the sunlight, a gentle sunlight powerless but to lend their soft white skin a rosy glow.

Two of them are lying down. The first has her feet in the air and her heels pressed to the trunk of the walnut tree in a posture of abandon suited to indoors, revealing that the young women believe themselves to be utterly alone. The second has her head in the lap of a third and is toying with a hat, whose embroidered brim she spins with her fingers. As she speaks, the hat turns, and this is Samuel's first sight of her—or at least, that's how I've always heard it from my mother, who got the details of the scene not only from her father, Samuel himself, but also from her own mother, who often said, my mother would tell me, that because of the hat she was balancing on her right hand, spinning the brim between the thumb and index finger of her left, she didn't see him coming but guessed it from the expression on the face of the fourth girl, who at that moment is emerging from behind a bush, readjusting her underwear, the hitched-up sides of her long skirt spilling over her arms, and is about to say something to her friends when all of a sudden she sees a man on horseback stopped not ten paces away. My future grandmother realizes what is going on, straightens up at once, and finds herself sitting, buttocks by her heels, torso upright, utterly parallel to that of her friend on whose lap she was laying her head, while the one whose legs had been raised in the air sits up sharply, pulling her dress over her legs in a hurry. And all four of them are now looking at the man on horseback, or rather the men, because another rider has just appeared behind the first. Samuel, embarrassed at having caught this intimate scene off guard, greets them politely, doffing his hat, and in doing so, notes the parasol open on the ground as well as a few wicker picnic baskets full of victuals indicating that a breakfast in the countryside is in the offing.

*

And so he greets them and says a few words in apology. But the four girls do not make a move, they respond with a very discreet greeting and wait to see what he will do next. Samuel then asks if this is the right way to Rashaya. Two of the young women—the one who was used as a headrest, and the one who emerged from behind the bush—ask him whom he's looking for in Rashaya. Talal mentions his cousin, Fayyad al-Atrash. The girls recognize the name, and naturally the mood relaxes, such that the young woman with the hat, my future grandmother, is then able to inquire about where these gentlemen came from, and she deftly uses the word *khawaja*, which might seem ironic, for no one would call an adventurer who turns up out of the blue in the hills of lower Hermon *khawaja*, not even if he is wearing a city dweller's hat. But above all what Samuel hears in this word is, beyond a shadow of a doubt, the accent of a daughter of the Beirut bourgeoisie, for in Rashaya as in all mountain regions, the first vowel is most likely elided: *khwaja*. Moreover, everything about the young woman confirms this impression—her hair swept back like earflaps from her temples, her dress and the white stockings she alone wears, her low-heeled shoes. She also gives off an impression of cleverness, though she remains guarded, and her eyes are limpid as the early autumn light. All in all, she is quite pretty, as her photos from the time attest, and Samuel replies that he has come from far away, from the Sudan, Egypt, and Arabia across the desert. She gives him a quick, intent stare and declares that he looks neither like a Bedouin nor a caravaner. Still mounted, Samuel launches into the same old story: that he is a merchant bringing goods to Beirut. But my grandmother—according to what she told her daughter, my mother, who told me the whole story much later— did not believe a word of it. A trader from Arabia doesn't gallivant about in a military uniform, with an aristocrat's mustache, treating himself to a day in the country, followed by a fierce bodyguard. It occurs to her that he may be a British agent, guided by a Druze resistance fighter, or something just as intriguing or romantic. But she doesn't say a thing, just watches with her fluid gaze, the twinkle in which she has completely mastered, and so it falls to my grandfather to ask what the situation is like in Rashaya.

As she answers, she opens one of the wicker baskets and takes out bread wrapped in thick cloth napkins, jars of olives, and small cucumbers. As if this were a sign, her three friends, who are undoubtedly local girls serving as traveling companions, see to the other baskets, unfurling a tablecloth on the ground, clearing away old walnuts fallen from the branches, and all of this seems a silent, indolent invitation to the two men to share their breakfast. After a moment's hesitation, Samuel dares to dismount at last, followed by Talal, the swaggering hero who hasn't said a single word since he mentioned his cousin and who seems oddly shy and embarrassed. They both approach, then sit down—not, in theory, to eat, not at all, just to keep the conversation going. But finally they do the meal justice and eat the *labneh*, the black olives and the green, the sheep cheese and the goat, reaching out, serving themselves with their fingers even as they speak. To one question about the goods he's bringing from so far away, Samuel replies that this is an Arab palace in a thousand pieces and marble deities. The girls laugh, the pretty city dweller declares she would have liked to see that, Talal grins under his mustache, and Samuel reflects that there are two ways of entering the promised land: the first consists of mounting an assault and slaughtering its inhabitants, and the second of having, upon arrival, a picnic just as in paradise.

After an hour, he has learned about the young bourgeois girl everything he will later have all the time in the world to come to know in greater depth, which is to say—her name is Émilie, she is the daughter of a rich Beiruti doctor, and she spends her every summer in Rashaya, including this one, which is drawing to an end since she is leaving for the capital the next morning. Shelling walnuts on a rock in front of him and passing the meat to the four young women, he brings up the automobile parked a bit farther off, and now a minor feminine commotion ensues. The four pretty women trade knowing glances, murmur things from which Samuel deduces that they were unaware of the nearby car, and Émilie announces that obviously her uncle has had her followed again; he is always afraid for her no matter what, he is responsible for her in the absence of her father, who has been stuck in Alexandria for three years and so has her kept under close watch at all times. "Not as close as all that," Samuel says, and so to prove it to him—or so Émilie will tell her daughter, my mother—she calls out toward the surrounding trees and now a small man appears, embarrassed, discreet, and slightly amused, in European shirt and slacks, with a smart bushy mustache; he comes forward, apologizing, it's not my fault, I had my instructions, you must believe me, *ya sitt Imilie, ya sitt Imilie*. Émilie smiles, shrugging, the other young women invite the bodyguard to sit down and eat, Samuel hands him a walnut, but the man politely declines, wishing only to withdraw, to go and hide again, for lack of a door to close behind him and leave this gathering to its privacy. But he has broken the spell, and they decide to pack up. After which, it is an odd group indeed that heads for the automobile: four young women with parasols, two horsemen leading their mounts behind them, and a bodyguard-chauffeur out in front, as if to blaze a trail, or else show the way, who winds up going ahead to warm up the engine.

Next, it is the two riders who take off at a gallop, leaving the car to crawl along cautiously behind, as there is no road for it, only hills of gravelly dirt sown with holm oak and pines in which it seems to have lost its way. By afternoon, Samuel and Talal are back at their camp, along with Fayyad al-Atrash. At dusk, instead of giving the signal to depart, Samuel sends his men off to sleep, announcing that they will leave at dawn, despite incomprehension from Talal and his cousin, a big strapping lad in a sirwal, with a grating accent. And indeed, they set out shortly before dawn, such that they reach the valley floor by midmorning. Then, instead of staying among the hills, as prudence demands, Samuel has the caravan hug the track toward Zahlé, just behind a curtain of small mountains that hide it from view. He himself, accompanied by his puzzled Druze abadays, remains on the ridge above the fields of mown wheat and the road on which only lazy mule-drivers and goatherders are to be found in the morning calm, letting out odd harmonics and clicks of the tongue to keep their animals from straying. But to the south, the automobile appears at last, in a cloud of dust that haloes it and betrays its presence from a distance like a banner. There can be no other automobiles in the area, and so Samuel hurries down to meet it, followed by his companions. The car, topped by a load of three trunks that crown it with a kind of top hat or stovepipe, rolls along at a brisk pace despite the road's rocks and ruts, which send it leaping and dancing. In a few minutes, it draws abreast of the riders who surround it and escort it, spurring their mounts ever faster so the car does not outpace its joyful honor guard. In the car, Émilie has immediately figured out who these men are, but she lets the race go on, laughing, delighting, and clapping like a child who has finally spotted the friends come to free her from the yoke of her bodyguards and tutors. Such that at the moment when her chauffeur finally slows so as not to hit one of the riders, then prudently comes to a halt as the dust settles and the sound of the motor dies away, Samuel Ayyad leans through the window and greets Émilie, doffing his hat, and she declares with a broad smile that she is really very happy to see him again.

On her way back to Beirut, Émilie is accompanied by her driver, one of the three girls from the day before, who seems to be officially in her service or her family's, and a gentleman who seems like a tutor or a secretary, in a European suit, a subject of her empire who dares not confront her and make her hear the voice of what he believes is reason or proper conduct. And as Samuel is now playing the role of a highwayman intercepting a car on the open road, he, too, will be someone who speaks against reason and what might pass for proper conduct—which is doubtless why she will love him. When

she sets foot on land, a bit unsteady as if stepping from
the deck of a ship after a stormy crossing, he tells her
that he has been waiting to show her his famous cargo,
much like a charmer who proposes in some suggestive
way that a conquest come see his collection of prints or
idols. She gladly agrees and takes a horse from one of
the Druze abadays from the Hauran, who shows courtesy for the occasion despite the fierce air about him, his
billhook mustache, and his necklace of rifle cartridges.
She mounts quite nimbly, despite her flowered dress
which she lifts to straddle her mount and sit on a saddle rug decorated with virile amulets. Five minutes later,
from atop a hill, she spots the endlessly unreeling line
of animals with their burdens. Next Samuel leads her
along the caravan, then gives the order to stop and, right
there, amidst the dry hills dotted with sturdy little trees,
unwrap the thousand pieces of the palace as well as the
pantheon. And with her on foot now, the secretary who
has caught up with them following a polite three paces
behind, they stroll through the display of fragmented
splendors, frescoed walls, mirrors, chimneys, Oriental
glories mingling with the backsides of mules and horses
growing impatient and men shouting conflicting orders
as they unload. After a moment, she winds up asking
him what he will do with these treasures once in Beirut,
and unhesitatingly he replies, with a shiver at his own
audacity, that he will reconstruct the palace so he can
live in it with her. Dumbfounded, Émilie turns what she

hopes is a mocking face his way, but blushes as she meets his eyes, looks away and, laughing, incredulous, continues her stroll, dragging him along as if nothing had happened. On the hills all around, like lookouts, the Druzes have dismounted and are waiting, sitting cross-legged while the mule-drivers and the peasants finish unwrapping. A shepherd off to one side stares at all the bustle, chin resting on his staff, letting his goats run about as he no doubt does when they graze in the ruins of ancient temples, leaving their droppings on the mosaics of flora and fauna.

*

When she has seen it all, Émilie, instead of returning to her car, bids it follow and for the rest of the day—that is, till Zahlé, the caravan's final stop before Beirut—she rides on horseback beside Samuel. And once again Samuel feels that his wanderings are over, that he has truly come home. This fills him with tremendous relief, and at the same time the barest hint of melancholy, a feeling of abiding friendship for the memory of the wanderers and nomads with whom he has shared his life, for the caravaners with eyes weathered from scanning distant horizons, for the women in their bobbing palanquins and the ones walking beside their men, arms and ankles ringed in golden bracelets, whose skirts the wind sometimes lifts, making them laugh, for the wind that puts fires to sleep and swells tents by rushing shamelessly into them, for the indigent tents of minor chieftains and the brocaded, stately tents of patriarchs, for feasts of greasy rice and meat, for the sentinels who keep watch by doused fires beneath the cold embers of the night sky, for the umbrella-like trees of the savannah, for the desert's mountainous sculptures, for your shadow which walks between your feet, for the meals of dates and nauseating boiled camel, for the lukewarm well water which must be drunk despite its metallic taste, because there is no choice, but also for dawns clear as spring water and the days' sweltering heat, for crimson dusks and for the night that falls so swiftly on the great book of sand of the deserts and savannahs of forgetful memory.

CHARIF MAJDALANI, born in Lebanon in 1960, is often compared to a Lebanese Proust. Majdalani lived in France from 1980 to 1993 and now teaches French literature at the Université Saint-Joseph in Beirut. The original French version of *Moving the Palace* won the 2008 François Mauriac Prize from the Académie Française as well as the Prix Tropiques.

EDWARD GAUVIN has received prizes and fellowships including those awarded by PEN America, the National Endowment for the Arts and the Fulbright program. His work has won the John Dryden Translation Prize and the Science Fiction & Fantasy Translation Award. He has translated over 200 graphic novels.

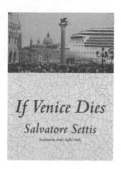

IF VENICE DIES BY SALVATORE SETTIS

INTERNATIONALLY RENOWNED ART HISTORIAN Salvatore Settis ignites a new debate about the Pearl of the Adriatic and cultural patrimony at large. In this fiery blend of history and cultural analysis, Settis argues that "hit-and-run" visitors are turning Venice and other landmark urban settings into shopping malls and theme parks. This is a passionate plea to secure the soul of Venice, written with consummate authority, wide-ranging erudition and élan.

A VERY RUSSIAN CHRISTMAS

THIS IS RUSSIAN CHRISTMAS CELEBRATED IN supreme pleasure and pain by the greatest of writers, from Dostoevsky and Tolstoy to Chekhov and Teffi. The dozen stories in this collection will satisfy every reader, and with their wit, humor, and tenderness, packed full of sentimental songs, footmen, whirling winds, solitary nights, snow drifts, and hopeful children, the collection proves that Nobody Does Christmas Like the Russians.

THE MADONNA OF NOTRE DAME BY ALEXIS RAGOUGNEAU

FIFTY THOUSAND PEOPLE JAM INTO NOTRE DAME Cathedral to celebrate the Feast of the Assumption. The next morning, a beautiful young woman clothed in white kneels at prayer in a cathedral side chapel. But when someone accidentally bumps against her, her body collapses. She has been murdered. This thrilling novel illuminates shadowy corners of the world's most famous cathedral, shedding light on good and evil with suspense, compassion and wry humor.

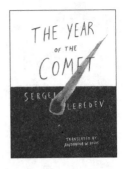

THE YEAR OF THE COMET
BY SERGEI LEBEDEV

A STORY OF A RUSSIAN BOYHOOD AND COMING of age as the Soviet Union is on the brink of collapse. Lebedev depicts a vast empire coming apart at the seams, transforming a very public moment into something tender and personal, and writes with stunning beauty and shattering insight about childhood and the growing consciousness of a boy in the world.

ADUA BY IGIABA SCEGO

ADUA, AN IMMIGRANT FROM SOMALIA TO ITALY, has lived in Rome for nearly forty years. She came seeking freedom from a strict father and an oppressive regime, but her dreams of film stardom ended in shame. Now that the civil war in Somalia is over, her homeland calls her. She must decide whether to return and reclaim her inheritance, but also how to take charge of her own story and build a future.

THE 6:41 TO PARIS
BY JEAN-PHILIPPE BLONDEL

CÉCILE, A STYLISH 47-YEAR-OLD, HAS SPENT THE weekend visiting her parents outside Paris. By Monday morning, she's exhausted. These trips back home are stressful and she settles into a train compartment with an empty seat beside her. But it's soon occupied by a man she recognizes as Philippe Leduc, with whom she had a passionate affair that ended in her brutal humiliation 30 years ago. In the fraught hour and a half that ensues, Cécile and Philippe hurtle towards the French capital in a psychological thriller about the pain and promise of past romance.

ON THE RUN WITH MARY
BY JONATHAN BARROW

SHINING MOMENTS OF TENDER BEAUTY PUNC-
tuate this story of a youth on the run after
escaping from an elite English boarding school.
At London's Euston Station, the narrator meets
a talking dachshund named Mary and together
they're off on escapades through posh Mayfair
streets and jaunts in a Rolls-Royce. But the
youth soon realizes that the seemingly sweet dog
is a handful; an alcoholic, nymphomaniac, drug-addicted mess who can't
stay out of pubs or off the dance floor. *On the Run with Mary* mirrors the
horrors and the joys of the terrible 20th century.

OBLIVION BY SERGEI LEBEDEV

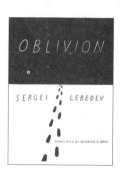

IN ONE OF THE FIRST 21ST CENTURY RUSSIAN
novels to probe the legacy of the Soviet prison
camp system, a young man travels to the vast
wastelands of the Far North to uncover the
truth about a shadowy neighbor who saved his
life, and whom he knows only as Grandfather
II. Emerging from today's Russia, where the ills
of the past are being forcefully erased from public memory, this masterful novel represents an
epic literary attempt to rescue history from the brink of oblivion.

THE LAST WEYNFELDT
BY MARTIN SUTER

ADRIAN WEYNFELDT IS AN ART EXPERT IN AN
international auction house, a bachelor in his
mid-fifties living in a grand Zurich apartment
filled with costly paintings and antiques. Always
correct and well-mannered, he's given up on
love until one night—entirely out of character for him—Weynfeldt decides to take home
a ravishing but unaccountable young woman
and gets embroiled in an art forgery scheme that threatens his buttoned
up existence. This refined page-turner moves behind elegant bourgeois
facades into darker recesses of the heart.

THE LAST SUPPER BY KLAUS WIVEL

ALARMED BY THE OPPRESSION OF 7.5 MILLION Christians in the Middle East, journalist Klaus Wivel traveled to Iraq, Lebanon, Egypt, and the Palestinian territories to learn about their fate. He found a minority under threat of death and humiliation, desperate in the face of rising Islamic extremism and without hope their situation will improve. An unsettling account of a severely beleaguered religious group living, so it seems, on borrowed time. Wivel asks, Why have we not done more to protect these people?

GUYS LIKE ME BY DOMINIQUE FABRE

DOMINIQUE FABRE, BORN IN PARIS AND A LIFE-long resident of the city, exposes the shadowy, anonymous lives of many who inhabit the French capital. In this quiet, subdued tale, a middle-aged office worker, divorced and alienated from his only son, meets up with two childhood friends who are similarly adrift. He's looking for a second act to his mournful life, seeking the harbor of love and a true connection with his son. Set in palpably real Paris streets that feel miles away from the City of Light, a stirring novel of regret and absence, yet not without a glimmer of hope.

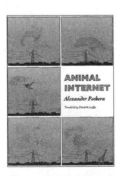

ANIMAL INTERNET BY ALEXANDER PSCHERA

SOME 50,000 CREATURES AROUND THE GLOBE—including whales, leopards, flamingoes, bats and snails—are being equipped with digital tracking devices. The data gathered and studied by major scientific institutes about their behavior will warn us about tsunamis, earthquakes and volcanic eruptions, but also radically transform our relationship to the natural world. Contrary to pessimistic fears, author Alexander Pschera sees the Internet as creating a historic opportunity for a new dialogue between man and nature.

KILLING AUNTIE BY ANDRZEJ BURSA

A YOUNG UNIVERSITY STUDENT NAMED JUREK, with no particular ambitions or talents, finds himself with nothing to do. After his doting aunt asks the young man to perform a small chore, he decides to kill her for no good reason other than, perhaps, boredom. This short comedic masterpiece combines elements of Dostoevsky, Sartre, Kafka, and Heller, coming together to produce an unforgettable tale of murder and—just maybe—redemption.

I CALLED HIM NECKTIE BY MILENA MICHIKO FLAŠAR

TWENTY-YEAR-OLD TAGUCHI HIRO HAS SPENT the last two years of his life living as a hikikomori—a shut-in who never leaves his room and has no human interaction—in his parents' home in Tokyo. As Hiro tentatively decides to reenter the world, he spends his days observing life from a park bench. Gradually he makes friends with Ohara Tetsu, a salaryman who has lost his job. The two discover in their sadness a common bond. This beautiful novel is moving, unforgettable, and full of surprises.

WHO IS MARTHA? BY MARJANA GAPONENKO

IN THIS ROLLICKING NOVEL, 96-YEAR-OLD ornithologist Luka Levadski foregoes treatment for lung cancer and moves from Ukraine to Vienna to make a grand exit in a luxury suite at the Hotel Imperial. He reflects on his past while indulging in Viennese cakes and savoring music in a gilded concert hall. Levadski was born in 1914, the same year that Martha—the last of the now-extinct passenger pigeons—died. Levadski himself has an acute sense of being the last of a species. This gloriously written tale mixes piquant wit with lofty musings about life, friendship, aging and death.

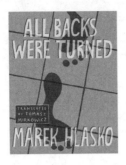

ALL BACKS WERE TURNED
BY MAREK HLASKO

TWO DESPERATE FRIENDS—ON THE EDGE OF the law—travel to the southern Israeli city of Eilat to find work. There, Dov Ben Dov, the handsome native Israeli with a reputation for causing trouble, and Israel, his sidekick, stay with Ben Dov's younger brother, Little Dov, who has enough trouble of his own. Local toughs are encroaching on Little Dov's business, and he enlists his older brother to drive them away. It doesn't help that a beautiful German widow is rooming next door. A story of passion, deception, violence, and betrayal, conveyed in hard-boiled prose reminiscent of Hammett and Chandler.

ALEXANDRIAN SUMMER
BY YITZHAK GORMEZANO GOREN

THIS IS THE STORY OF TWO JEWISH FAMILIES LIVing their frenzied last days in the doomed cosmopolitan social whirl of Alexandria just before fleeing Egypt for Israel in 1951. The conventions of the Egyptian upper-middle class are laid bare in this dazzling novel, which exposes sexual hypocrisies and portrays a vanished polyglot world of horse racing, seaside promenades and nightclubs.

COCAINE BY PITIGRILLI

PARIS IN THE 1920S—DIZZY AND DECADENT. Where a young man can make a fortune with his wits … unless he is led into temptation. Cocaine's dandified hero Tito Arnaudi invents lurid scandals and gruesome deaths, and sells these stories to the newspapers. But his own life becomes even more outrageous when he acquires three demanding mistresses. Elegant, witty and wicked, Pitigrilli's classic novel was first published in Italian in 1921 and retains its venom even today.

KILLING THE SECOND DOG
BY MAREK HLASKO

TWO DOWN-AND-OUT POLISH CON MEN LIVING in Israel in the 1950s scam an American widow visiting the country. Robert, who masterminds the scheme, and Jacob, who acts it out, are tough, desperate men, exiled from their native land and adrift in the hot, nasty underworld of Tel Aviv. Robert arranges for Jacob to run into the widow who has enough trouble with her young son to keep her occupied all day. What follows is a story of romance, deception, cruelty and shame. Hlasko's writing combines brutal realism with smoky, hard-boiled dialogue, in a bleak world where violence is the norm and love is often only an act.

FANNY VON ARNSTEIN: DAUGHTER OF
THE ENLIGHTENMENT BY HILDE SPIEL

IN 1776 FANNY VON ARNSTEIN, THE DAUGHTER of the Jewish master of the royal mint in Berlin, came to Vienna as an 18-year-old bride. She married a financier to the Austro-Hungarian imperial court, and hosted an ever more splendid salon which attracted luminaries of the day. Spiel's elegantly written and carefully researched biography provides a vivid portrait of a passionate woman who advocated for the rights of Jews, and illuminates a central era in European cultural and social history.

SOME DAY BY SHEMI ZARHIN

ON THE SHORES OF ISRAEL'S SEA OF GALILEE lies the city of Tiberias, a place bursting with sexuality and longing for love. The air is saturated with smells of cooking and passion. Some Day is a gripping family saga, a sensual and emotional feast that plays out over decades. This is an enchanting tale about tragic fates that disrupt families and break our hearts. Zarhin's hypnotic writing renders a painfully delicious vision of individual lives behind Israel's larger national story.

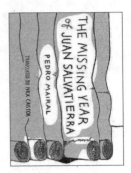

THE MISSING YEAR OF JUAN SALVATIERRA
BY PEDRO MAIRAL

AT THE AGE OF NINE, JUAN SALVATIERRA BECAME mute following a horse riding accident. At twenty, he began secretly painting a series of canvases on which he detailed six decades of life in his village on Argentina's frontier with Uruguay. After his death, his sons return to deal with their inheritance: a shed packed with rolls over two miles long. But an essential roll is missing. A search ensues that illuminates links between art and life, with past family secrets casting their shadows on the present.

THE GOOD LIFE ELSEWHERE
BY VLADIMIR LORCHENKOV

THE VERY FUNNY—AND VERY SAD—STORY OF A group of villagers and their tragicomic efforts to emigrate from Europe's most impoverished nation to Italy for work. An Orthodox priest is deserted by his wife for an art-dealing atheist; a mechanic redesigns his tractor for travel by air and sea; and thousands of villagers take to the road on a modern-day religious crusade to make it to the Italian Promised Land. A country where 25 percent of its population works abroad, remittances make up nearly 40 percent of GDP, and alcohol consumption per capita is the world's highest – Moldova surely has its problems. But, as Lorchenkov vividly shows, it's also a country whose residents don't give up easily.

 New Vessel Press

*To purchase these titles and for more information
please visit newvesselpress.com.*